AIDAN

MADMAN MACKEEFE SERIES - BOOK 2

ELIZABETH ROSE

ROSESCRIBE MEDIA INC.

CHAPTER 1

MadMan MacKeefe Series

*O*nly a madman would use a stone for his pillow. The Stone of Destiny to be precise.

Aidan MacKeefe tossed restlessly in his sleep, having used the Stone of Destiny as his pillow for the last six months now, hoping to have prophetic dreams. Supposedly, the stone was used back in the days of the Bible, and Jacob had used this exact stone and had dreams of angels.

Aidan was in the middle of a dream. Mist surrounded him in his little stone cottage in the MacKeefe camp. He couldn't see anything in the darkened room, but then the door opened, and in the bright light – he saw an angel. The angel walked toward him, covered with a long, white, hooded cloak, her fiery red tresses falling in ringlets down to her shoulders. Stopping in front of him, she peeked out from under the hood. While he couldn't see her face well in the dark, he could still see her wide, green eyes that reminded him of the color of the moors on a warm summer's day. Her gaze steadied upon him and she lit a candle in her hand, illuminating her face beneath the hood.

Her skin was fair, like alabaster, and a smattering of fine freckles trailed down her nose and spread to her rosy cheeks. Aye, she was a bonnie lass, and though he couldn't see her body under the robe, he was sure it matched her beauty. He wanted her badly. Then she smiled at him, and her laugh rang out across the room like the sweet song of a small meadow pipit, bringing with it a fragile innocence to its tone. She was a fine angel. A perfect Scottish angel. He wanted naught more than to reach out his hands and touch her, but something weighted him down and he could not move.

As she reached out to him, he saw a strawberry birthmark on the inside of her arm that looked like . . . a skull. He felt himself jerk away from her touch, and then she turned away from him and nodded toward the door. Aidan's attention focused across the small room, and to his horror he saw English soldiers following her into the cottage with their weapons drawn.

Aidan tried to cry out for help, but couldn't speak. He tried to reach for his sword at his side, but couldn't move. Then his eyes scanned down her body, and to his horror, he saw sticking out from the back of her robe right by her doup – a tail. A furry red tail! It reached out and brushed across his face, and in his only form of defense he leaned forward . . . and bit it.

The sickening screech of an animal cried out, pulling him from his slumber. His eyes popped open, bringing him out of the dream and he sat up quickly, not knowing what was happening.

Then he saw Reid, his pet red squirrel scurrying off his chest, scolding him, running in circles around the room. The door opened just then, but instead of his dream angel, his friend, Ian, stood there with a dour expression upon his face.

"What in the clootie's name was thet screech?" asked Ian. His tall, muscular form filled the entire doorway, and his dark hair looked wet as if he'd just come from bathing in the loch.

Aidan jumped up, realizing he was fully clothed, and that it was well into the morning hours. Then he remembered taking a nap, too full to move after eating his fill of skirlie, an oatmeal and onion dish topped off with a goose egg. The food for the clan had been prepared by his younger sister, Kyla, and the chieftain's wife, Wren.

The door pushed open from behind Ian, and there stood their good friend, Onyx, who had recently married an Englishwoman, Lady Lovelle of Worcestershire, after finding out that his true family was English, not Scottish at all.

"Aidan, ye dunderheid," said Onyx, spying the squirrel running around the room in a heated frenzy. Onyx's two different colored eyes stared back at him in question. "What did ye do te yer squirrel?"

"I think I bit its tail," he said, running a hand through his hair and leaning back against the stone. The Stone of Scone, or Stone of Destiny as most called it, was a large, black basalt rock with ancient hieroglyphs etched into it. It had iron-looped handles embedded into the sides to use for carrying with a pole through it. The stone was very heavy, and took at least two full-grown men to move it - if they were strong. He'd embedded the thick stone into the dirt of the cottage floor to lower it, and pulled his pallet over it,

to use as his personal pillow.

"Were ye hungry so soon after eatin' so much skirlie?" asked Ian, walking into the room and sitting down. Onyx followed, leaving the door wide open. The summer sun spilled into the cottage, lighting it up and bringing with it a fresh breeze from the Highland hills.

"Nay, I had a dream." Aidan settled himself atop the stone and donned his leather shoes that laced around his legs. Highlanders often went barefooted in the summer, unless they were traveling, like they would be today. "She was a bonnie angel with reid hair, I tell ye."

"And so ye bit her?" asked Onyx, pulling up a chair and making himself comfortable. He raised an eyebrow in amusement, his one orange eye shining in the sun from the door, while his other black eye stayed in shadow. Most people thought Onyx was a madman because of his eyes. All three of the friends were madmen, and Aidan prided himself of the fact. If there were an outlandish or dangerous act or activity suggested, they were the first to try it just for excitement.

"Nay. Me Scottish angel had a tail – and we all ken thet our enemies have tails," he said, pointing out the superstition held throughout the lands. "And I couldna move, so I bit it."

Ian and Onyx both laughed hysterically, holding their sides and almost falling from their chairs.

"Ye big galoot," said Ian. "Yer squirrel must o' been sleepin' on yer chest again and ye bit its tail."

"Sorry, Reid," Aidan said, looking over to the other side of the room where his pet was sitting on the floor licking its wounds. "So Dagger," he continued, calling Onyx by the name only his close friends used, "when did ye get te the Highlands? I thought ye were visitin' yer new family in England fer awhile."

"I jest arrived," Onyx told him. "Actually, Love is stayin' with her mathair fer awhile in Worcestershire," he said, speaking about his wife. "E'er since she started gettin' heavy with our bairn-te-be, she seems te want te be close to her mathair. Since I'm no' her new faither's favorite as he still hates Scots, we decided I'd be best off visitin' the MacKeefes until she's closer te birthin' the bairn."

"I canna picture ye being a faither," said Aidan.

"I already am a faither te her son, Charles."

"So is Charles with her then?" Ian inspected a wooden cup on the table and smelled it, then decided to sample its contents. He made a face and set the cup back down quickly.

"Nay." Onyx leaned back on two legs of the chair, with his

arms crossed and also stretching out his feet atop the small table. "The lad wanted te go back te Blackpool and be fostered by me own faither as they are gettin' along nicely, and I do believe the lad enjoys being a page. Someday he'll make a fine squire."

"And how are *ye* gettin' along with yer faither?" asked Aidan, knowing Onyx still had some ill feelings for the man who almost killed him as a baby.

"We are gettin' along better e'ery day," he relayed. "I even invited him te join us at the Highland Games in the fall."

The Highland Games was a tradition of many different competitions, and everyone looked forward to it.

"Guid," said Aidan, reaching over and picking up his sword. He laid it across his lap and shined it with the edge of his purple and green plaid. The clan's old weaver only knew how to weave one pattern, so the plaids of the MacKeefes ended up all looking the same. "Guid, thet is, thet he'll be able te see me win the caber toss and also beat ye inte the ground with the sword hold."

"Aidan, keep dreamin' on thet rock o' yers, because ye're daft," said Onyx. "Ye'll ne'er beat me at the sword hold, and ye ken it. I can hold swords high and proud to me sides all day and night if I have te, and you'll ne'er see me arms shakin' at all."

"Aye, thet's true," agreed Ian with a nod of his head. "He can. And Aidan, what makes ye think ye can beat our chieftain at the caber toss? E'eryone kens thet Storm has held the title o' winnin' the caber toss fer the last nine years now. He is countin' on makin' it te ten and havin' a huge celebration."

"That's right," said Wren, Storm's English wife, as she appeared in the open doorway with Kyla, Aidan's sister at her side. "My husband is King of the Caber, and you all know it's because I'm his good luck charm." Wren was a few years over thirty, and she and their laird had four children. Wren's long, black hair was tied up and covered with a kertch as was custom of married women.

"Aye, brathair," said Kyla. "Ye canna beat Storm." Kyla pulled her long, light-brown hair back, tying it with a ribbon as she spoke.

"Well, then I jest need a guid luck charm also," said Aidan, standing up with his sword in his hand.

"Ye jest dreamt o' one on thet stone pillow o' yers," said Ian with a smile. "Tail and all."

Onyx and Ian started laughing again, and Aidan threw down his sword and lunged at them, knocking Onyx off the chair and to the ground. Ian, in his usual form, wasted no time in getting Aidan into a headlock.

"Stop it, you three, and tell me what this is all about." Wren stood with her arms crossed over her chest, waiting for an explanation.

"Aidan was tryin' te dream up a lassie again, usin' the Stone o' Destiny," explained Onyx, pushing up to a standing position and brushing himself off.

"I was no'," said Aidan, stuck under Ian's armpit. Then, reaching backwards, he got a hold of his friend and flipped him over his head. Ian landed atop the table with a crash, and Onyx jumped out of the way of being hit. The squirrel chattered away, finding safety atop the Stone of Destiny.

"Then what *were* ye doin' takin' a nap in the middle o' the day?" asked Onyx.

"'Tis no' the middle o' the day," grumbled Aidan. "And I was tryin' te have visions in me sleep, the way Jacob did in the Bible."

"Ye ken ye three are supposed to be guardin' thet stone, not usin' it te find lassies te bed," said Kyla, squinting and looking at them out of one eye. She was six years younger than her brother, at nine and ten years of age, but still, she'd kept up with Aidan and his friends her entire life. Kyla was always around them, wanting to be part of whatever danger they were getting themselves into. She wasn't close to any of the women of the clan and considered herself more, 'one of the boys.'

"I take me position of guardian o' the stone seriously," said Aidan, going back and sitting atop the stone.

"Only someone with rocks in their heid would sleep on the damned thing," muttered Ian, sliding off the table and getting to his feet.

"The stone is only in our possession until the end of the year," Wren reminded them. "After that, it'll go in secret to another clan to protect it, so the English never find out that their king stole a fake coronation stone so many years ago. This system has worked well for the last five and sixty years, so don't ruin it."

"Dagger, ye didna tell Lovelle about it, did ye?" asked Ian. "Or any o' yer family? After all, they are all English and if their king finds out the English have stolen a fake coronation stone, he'll send his armies after it, sooner or later."

"I didna say a word te me English family," said Onyx. "Only Love kens, but she willna tell the rest o' them."

"Ye shouldna o' told her," said Aidan.

"She is me wife. I can trust her." Onyx raised his palms in the air and shrugged as he spoke.

"She's also a Sassenach. Ye can only really trust the Scots thet our stone is in safe hidin'," Aidan reminded him.

Wren cleared her throat just then and shook her head. "I am English as well as Storm's mother, so I am sure we can all trust that Scotland's secret is still safe. Now hurry up, as Storm sent me to tell you that everyone is ready to go to the trade fair in Glasgow, and we're just waiting for you three." She left the room with Kyla following right behind her, leaving the door open.

Aidan looked at the Stone of Destiny, having taken a personal guardianship over it these past six months. Back in 1296, King Edward I, stole the coronation stone from the Scots from an abbey in Scone. Little did the king know, the abbot had replaced it with a fake, large, red sandstone, and the real stone was safe in hiding.

Because the English weren't really familiar with what the

stone looked like, they had taken naught but a decoy. And with the Scots taking turns over guardianship and moving it from clan to clan, they'd managed to keep safe the stone used in every Scottish coronation since Kenneth MacAlpin, the first king of Scots who was crowned over five hundred years ago.

"Aidan, ye dinna need te worry about me wife tellin' secrets. After all, ye are the one who canna e'er haud yer wheesht," spat Onyx.

"Thet's right," agreed Ian, pushing back his dark, tousled hair. "Ye are the one who always opens yer big mouth and says things ye shouldna."

"Thet's no' true," he protested.

"Really?" Onyx crossed his arms over his chest. "Then how did Lovelle ken what I was goin' te do when I went te kill me faither? After all, ye and Ian were the only ones I told."

"And how about the time ye told Kyla I was the one who hid her clothes when she was bathin' in the loch?" pointed out Ian.

"She's me sister," Aidan said in self-defense. "I couldna let ye see her naked! And Dagger," he said, nodding toward Onyx, "I couldna let ye kill yer faither, as I kent ye woulda regretted it someday."

Onyx just shook his head and smiled. "Face it, Aidan, if anyone wants te ken gossip, they dinna go te the alewives te find a waggin' tongue, they come te ye instead."

"Well, I willna e'er tell anyone about the stone," he said, feeling a wee bit bad that everything his friends were saying was true.

"It's been safe so far, so mayhap ye are changin'," said Ian.

Just then, Onyx's wildcat slinked into the room with a dead chough, red-legged crow, in its mouth. It saw the squirrel scampering around and dropped the bird and lunged for Aidan's pet instead. The squirrel scurried up Aidan's arm and settled itself on his shoulder. Aidan ran a hand over the squirrel to soothe it, and stood to put distance between his pet and its stalker.

"Dagger, yer pet has grown since we last saw ye," said Ian.

"Aye," agreed Aidan. "I dinna think its safe te bring it around camp. There are bairns and livestock and sheep in the hills . . . and squirrels here." His squirrel agreed by scolding the wildcat from atop Aidan's shoulder, flicking its tail wildly.

"Nay, Tawpie willna harm them," Onyx said, scooping up the cat, now having to use both hands to hold her, as she was no longer a cute little kitten. The cat's eyes stayed fastened on the squirrel. "I have raised her from a bairn, and she is only bein' playful since she is still so young. She listens te me, so dinna fash yerself about it."

"Still, jest te play it safe, ye should keep her locked up," said Aidan.

"I willna lock up me pet any more than ye'll do the same te yers." Onyx held the cat to his chest protectively. "Besides, she's jest caught a bird so she willna be hungry fer awhile."

"What is takin' ye three so long?" asked their chieftain, Storm, walking into the hut, followed by Wren. Storm and his father both served as chieftains to the clan, and took turns staying at either the Highland camp, or the Lowland castle they'd claimed near the border, Hermitage Castle. Wren spied the dead bird on the ground and jumped back, startled.

"Dagger's pet is killin' off e'erythin' in sight," complained Aidan.

"No' so," Onyx replied. "And I willna lock her up."

"I canna endanger the clan nor the livestock," said Storm, shaking his head. The long blond braid at the side of his head swung slightly, and the cat tried to swipe out for it with its paw.

Storm scowled, but Wren reached over and took the cat in her arms. She had always had a way with animals and truly loved them. "I'll get Renard to keep an eye on Tawpie during your visit," said Wren, offering the services of their eldest son of eight and ten summers for the job. He was actually Storm's son from a previous marriage, but Wren had raised him as if he were her own. "He used to have a pet fox years ago, and loves animals. He'll keep the children safe, don't worry."

"Then Renard and Niall will stay here te watch the cat as well as watch o'er the stone while we're at the fair," said Storm. Niall was Renard's cousin and also best friend, as they were about the same age, Niall being a little younger. They'd both turned out to be excellent with handling weapons thanks to Storm, so the stone would be in good hands. Besides, since the English didn't even know it existed, it wasn't in any real danger anyway.

"Storm, you know how much the boys look forward to the fair," Wren reminded him.

"I'll stay," offered Onyx.

"Nay," said Storm. "I need ye three te help me sell and trade fer goods we need at camp. Ye three are the best at gettin' a guid, fair trade, and also the best prices, so ye'll come with. Renard and Niall will take watch fer now and they can still go te the fair in a few days time."

"I had a dream," said Aidan anxiously. "I'm no' sure what it means, but I saw the English comin' inte this cottage."

"No' another o' yer dreams," grumbled Storm, not believing in anything supernatural. "Last time ye had a dream, ye had all the lassies bathin' e'eryday because ye were sure if they didna, they were goin' te get the pox."

"Aye, but I enjoyed thet," said Ian with a smile.

"Nay, this is different," Aidan tried to explain. "This was so real, and I'm no' sure what the English were doin' here."

"Mayhap they were hunting bonnie lassies . . . with furry tails," said Ian, causing another fit of laughter between him and Onyx.

"Aye," said Onyx, trying to catch his breath. "Mayhap Aidan should stay on watch so he can bite them all in the tails when they arrive."

"Haud yer wheesht," snapped Aidan, pushing past them out

the door with his squirrel on his shoulder. They could make a jest of his dream, but somehow he knew that it was one of those visions like Jacob had so many years ago. Though he had no idea what the dream meant, he felt that his Scottish angel was in trouble and somehow needed his help.

CHAPTER 2

MadMan MacKeefe Series

LIDDEL CASTLE, SCOTTISH BORDER

*E*ffie MacDuff opened her eyes, hoping she'd only been having a bad dream. But when her vision focused on the bars in front of her small confinement, she realized the nightmare was real.

"Coira?" she cried out, looking around for her younger sister. The floor swayed underneath her, and to her horror, she realized she was hanging in an iron basket from the side of a castle. She rubbed the bump on her head, still feeling like her skull had been split open by the English soldier when he knocked her senseless after she'd tried to defend their gypsy camp.

"Effie?" she heard her sister's small voice, and turned to see that she, too, was hanging like a bird in a cage. "I'm scared."

Effie jumped to her feet, nearly hitting her head atop the grates of her confinement. She wasn't tall by any standards, and their cages were barbaric, crude and small. She looked down to see the English soldiers looking up at them and laughing. They were on display for all to see, and the thought of this sickened her as well as made her very angry.

"Let us out o' here!" Taking hold of the bars, she tried to shake herself free. She glanced down to her bedraggled clothes, now torn and dirty from her scuffle when the men attacked their camp. Relief washed through her when she realized the soldiers hadn't stolen the MacDuff brooch of her grandmother that held closed her arisaidh - the long cloth wrapped around her and fastened at her shoulder. The metal, round brooch was engraved with a lion embedded with an amethyst eye, holding up its paw with a sword. Around its head was the clan's motto, Deus Juvat, or God Assists. It was all she had left to remember her family by, since the death of her mother years ago. By the grace of God, her descendants had passed down to her the MacDuff brooch. So now all she had left was this, and Coira, her younger sister.

"You'll stay put until we get word to King Edward that we've caught the descendant of that traitorous bitch, Isabel MacDuff," sneered one of the guards.

"Effie, what are they talkin' about?" asked her sister from the iron cage beside her.

For her entire life of twenty years, Effie had lived the life of a gypsy, keeping the secret her dying mother had told her the day she lost her life birthing Coira. Effie had only been six years old at the time, but she knew her life was never going to be the same after what her mother confessed to her that day. She missed her mother dearly, and only wished she were here right now.

"Dinna worry about it," she told her sister. "I'll get us out o' here, I swear."

"But they took yer dagger as well as yer bow and arrows. We have no way te protect ourselves from these bluidy bastards."

"Coira, watch yer words, as they arena thet o' a proper lassie."

"Ye canna tell me thet when I learned e'ery foul word I ken from ye, big sister."

Effie knew this was the truth. She'd learned to fight to protect them, and had hardened her heart the day she lost her mother. Her mother had warned her that the English would find them some day. Although they were MacDuffs, they were also descendants of a woman who angered the English years ago, and now they were the ones who were going to pay for it.

"Where are we?" Effie called down to the guards.

"You're in Liddel Castle," the guard told her.

"But . . . thet's a Scottish castle," she said, knowing of its whereabouts just north of the English border.

"Not anymore. Lord Ralston the Bold has seized it, and I assure you he is English, not a wretched Scot."

"What do ye want from us?" she called down to the guards. Her heart thumped in her chest and she knew it didn't look good for either her or her sister. If she couldn't strike up some kind of bargain, they would most likely die in these cages. She only hoped they wouldn't be tortured, or perhaps kept in a cage for four years the way the English had done to her grandmother, Isabel MacDuff. "What did ye do with the rest o' our clan?"

"What clan?" asked one of the guards. "You mean that band of gypsies you travel with? Hah! That's no clan, they were nothing but common thieves and swindlers."

If she weren't in such a dire situation, she'd almost find that amusing, since that's exactly what she'd been thinking about the English. "They are our family. Now let me loose, I demand you." She pulled on the grates again, causing the cage to rattle. A crow settled itself atop her sister's cage, reaching its beak through the bars, just waiting to be able to peck their eyes from their bodies as soon as they were dead and shriveled from the sun. Her sister screamed and hid her face in her hands.

"You have no gypsy family anymore," the guard relayed. "They tried to attack us when we came for you and your sister, and we had to kill them all."

"Nay!" she cried, the anguish inside her starting to boil over. Her heart felt hollow, and she mourned for the lives of the gypsies that were taken, because they did naught but protect Effie and her sister since the death of her mother. "I'll kill ye bastards, e'ery one o' ye, I swear. Ye willna get away with this."

"Effie?" She looked over to see her sister crying, and she wanted nothing more than to gather her into her arms and comfort her the way she'd always done through the years. But she couldn't. She tried to reach through the grates, and her sister reached for her as well, but while their hands were close, they could not touch each other. "They're goin' te kill us, arena they?"

Effie's heart broke to see the fear in her sister's eyes. Though the girl was already four and ten years of age, she'd been weak and sickly most her life, and her heart was not strong. She often fell victim to fevers, and Effie could already see her sister's frail body shaking. Though it was summer, come nightfall her sister would be cold.

"Nay, stay strong," she told Coira. "They canna win unless we give in te them, and lose our will te live."

"Why are they doin' this?" she asked again. "What did we do te deserve this kind o' treatment?"

"We did nothin'," she explained. "'Twas an act o' our grand-mathair thet has them so roiled."

"I kennawhat ye mean."

"I'll take care o' it, now jest get some sleep."

She saw her sister's eyes closing, and she knew the girl was exhausted. Effie swore she'd do whatever it took to right this situation. No more MacDuffs would live in a cage in front of the public eye the way her grandmother had. Her mother had told her in order to ensure their safety, they had to keep their identity a secret. She had no idea how the English found out about them, after all these years of thinking Isabel MacDuff died without issue.

The gypsy man, Tasgall, walked into view, and suddenly it was clear what had happened. Since the English did naught to confine him, she was sure this man had spilled their secret.

"How does it feel te be up there?" Tasgall asked, and flashed a quick smile.

"Ye traitor," she called down and spit at him out of the cage. She never did trust the old coot, ever since the day she found him stealing food from one of the bairns. He was over forty years of age and had a big nose and beady eyes. Effie thought it was shameful to even call him a Scot after what he'd just done. "Why did ye do it? Why did ye tell the English our secret?"

"Because I have a secret too, me little bird. Only mine is one thet the English like. Ye see, I am a descendant of the Comyns. And in case yer mathair didna explain te ye, yer grandmathair was married to a Comyn before she decided te betray the English crown."

"Ye have it wrong, ye fool. Me grandmathair wasna the one te do the betrayin'. She was loyal to Robert the Bruce, and also her country. Too bad I couldna say the same fer the Comyns."

"Aye. Too bad thet Comyn and Bruce were enemies, but then again ye have The Bruce te thank fer killin' Red Comyn so many years ago, so mayhap he's te blame fer ye hangin' in thet cage after all. Jest like what happened te yer dear auld grandmathair."

Effie knew only too well what he was talking about. Her mother had explained their roots, and that Isabel had left her brother being fostered in England, as well as her husband who had befriended the English king, to crown Robert the Bruce at Scone, as was the hereditary right of a MacDuff. She was a very brave and honorable woman. If she hadn't been captured by the English, things might be different for Effie and her sister today.

Effie's father was from the MacDuff clan and had come to her mother to couple in secret. He was a coward though, or he would have done something about rejoining them with the clan. She actually felt no remorse the day she held her mother's hand and looked down at the dead body of the father she never knew on the bloody field after the Battle at Neville's Cross. As far as she was concerned, the man got what he'd deserved. She was only too glad that Coira never had to experience this, as he'd died before she was actually born.

"Tell me what ye want," she cried out to the Englishmen. "I'll do anythin' at all, but please, jest set me sister free. She is no' well, and canna be treated this way."

"Anything?" asked the guard, and Effie could already feel her skin crawling at the thought that he'd probably defile her. Still, she would say whatever it took to get him to release her from the cage, and then perhaps she'd have half a chance of fighting him off or coming up with a plan to free her sister.

"Ye ken what yer lord wants," said Tasgall to the guards.

"Aye," said one of the guards, nodding his head. "But I think we should have our way with the girl first. Lower her down," he ordered another of his men.

The cage was lowered slowly to the ground, and the guard twisted the key in the lock, releasing the hinged door. He opened it and grabbed her by the hair and pulled her out into the dusty courtyard. He had the look of lust in his eyes, and may have tried something if the lord of the castle hadn't walked out at that moment.

"Good, Dempster," he said to his captain of the guard. "I see you've got the wench ready to go. Now take her to the Glasgow fair immediately, and don't let her out of your sight."

"Lord Ralston," complained the guard. "I thought we could have a little fun with her first."

The man named Lord Ralston reached out and grabbed Effie by the chin. His grip was tight and she could feel the pressure biting into her flesh.

"I'll be the first one to have her once she's delivered to us the information we need. Now, Scotsman," he said, looking toward Tasgall, "where did ye say you heard talk of the Stone of Destiny?"

"I heard the Highlanders talkin' about it in the pub when they were well in their cups," Tasgall told him. "I think they have the real stone, and the one King Edward stole is only a fake."

"Just as I thought," said Lord Ralston, nodding his head. "For years I've believed the English had a fake stone but couldn't prove it. But now, with any luck we'll not only have proof, but the stone itself."

"Shall I send word to King Edward that we've found information that the English have been tricked years ago?" asked the guard.

"Nay, not yet. Not until the girl gets us the information of its whereabouts," said Lord Ralston, releasing his hand from her chin and running his fingers through her hair. "With her looks, any Scot will tell her whatever she wants to know. And with that MacDuff brooch she's wearing, all of the Scots will trust her."

Now Effie knew why they hadn't taken her brooch. It was the symbol of a brave Scottish woman that all the Scots revered. They were going to use such an iconic symbol against her. It turned her stomach to even think of it.

She pulled away from Lord Ralston, and held up a hand to block him from touching her again. That's when his fist shot through the air, and though she moved aside, he still clipped her on the jaw for her actions. She fell to the ground, hearing her sister screaming from up in the cage.

"You stupid wench," he growled. "Don't you see if you don't do as I command, you'll pay for it dearly?"

"Do whate'er ye want te me," she said. "I willna betray Scotland by givin' ye any information. It is me homeland and I will be as loyal to it as me grandmathair was."

"Can we take her now?" asked Dempster.

"I said no," he spat. "You will get the information I request," he warned Effie. "Because if not . . ." his eyes roamed upward and stopped as his gaze landed on her sister. "If not, then your sister will pay for your incompetence. First with her body . . . and then with her life."

Effie looked upward to see her sister was not sleeping after all. Instead, she was holding onto the bars of her prison, peering at Effie with all the hope in the world in her eyes. She was frightened, but also trying to be strong. She shook her head, tears flowing from her eyes.

Effie had been more like a mother to Coira than a sister, after the death of their mother. She would protect her with her life, and never allow harm to come to her. Coira was her only family now. Her only reason to live. And though it pained her to do anything against Scotland, she would do whatever it took to save her sister's life.

"I'll do it," she said, trying to ignore her sister's wailing from behind her. "Tell me what information ye need, and I will get it fer ye. Just dinna do anythin' te harm me sister."

CHAPTER 3

*A*idan stepped out of the Horn and Hoof pub in Glasgow, followed by Onyx and Ian. He had his squirrel on his shoulder, and held up a crumb, feeding it as he walked.

"God's eyes, Aidan," said Ian, following him out into the midst of the fair. "Are ye goin' te be sore at us fore'er jest fer teasin' ye about yer dream?"

"Aye," said Onyx. "We've already been here fer two days now and ye're still actin' like a bairn about the whole blame thing."

"I jest wish ye two would take me dreams seriously," said Aidan.

"We do," answered Onyx.

"Howe'er, it is a wee bit tryin' when ye tell us such a . . . tail," said Ian. Ian looked at Onyx and they both burst out laughing.

Onyx slapped Ian on the back. "Let's get another dram o' auld Callum's mountain magic."

"Guid idea," said Ian. "Aidan, are ye goin' te join us?"

"Nay. I'm goin' te take Reid to the forest te root around. I'll meet ye back at the pub in a wee bit."

He headed off toward the edge of the forest, in no mood to drink with his friends. It wasn't usually like him to stay sore at them for so long, but something about the dream had him feeling very unsettled inside. Although he couldn't really remember the face of his angel anymore, one thing about the dream did not fade from his mind. The English soldiers in his cottage. He wondered if it was some sort of warning.

"Go on, Reid, and root around but hurry back." He put his squirrel on the ground, and the animal took off to the treetops. He sat down at the base of the tree and had only closed his eyes for a few moments when the squirrel started screeching, telling him that something was wrong.

Aidan opened his eyes and looked around, then heard a noise coming from deeper in the forest. It sounded like the voice of a woman, and it sounded as if she were in trouble. Grabbing his sword from his side, he jumped up and rushed through the forest.

"LET GO O' me ye brute," Effie said to the English guard, Dempster, who was trying hard to accost her. He was supposed to just bring her to the fair so she could find out information, but unfortunately, she could see that he had other plans. Especially when his friend appeared to help.

"I'll hold her for you, and you hold her for me," said the second guard, approaching quickly. Dempster threw her to the ground and his friend straddled her, pulling up the end of his tunic as he did so, untying his hose.

"Get off o' me, ye bastards!" She bit Dempster in the hand, and the second guard reached out to hit her, but was stopped by the strong fist of a Scottish Highlander as he shot out from the forest and twisted the man's wrist. Her attacker cried out in pain and she heard the bones in his hand snap.

"Get away from the lassie afore I kill ye," the Scotsman warned.

Dempster released her quickly, unsheathing his sword at his

side. The Scotsman met him with his own sword, and when the second guard stood to join him, the Highlander kicked him, sending him sprawling across the ground.

Effie jumped up and backed away from the fight, seeing the second guard pulling his sword and rushing toward the Scot.

"Behind ye," she cried out, and with one motion the Scot disarmed Dempster and had the point of his sword under the chin of the Englishman's friend.

"Did they harm ye in any way, lassie?" asked the Scot. "Because if they did, jest tell me and I'll run me blade through both o' them right now."

"Nay," she said, not wanting the guards killed, knowing that if that happened, Lord Ralston would probably take it out on her sister. "They didna harm me, now please jest let them go."

"Are ye sure?" he asked over his shoulder, but not taking his eyes from the men.

"I'm sure."

"Then I want the two of ye te leave quickly and no' come back te the fair. If I ever see ye again, I swear it'll be the last time we e'er meet, and it's no' me own deith I'm talkin' about."

The guards looked at her, and since she knew the Scot couldn't see her, she just nodded her head, signaling to them that she'd try to get information out of the Highlander.

"Fine," said Dempster. "Just let us go."

The Scot moved his blade from the soldier's neck and they both scurried away quickly out of sight.

"Thank ye," said Effie, when the man turned to look at her.

"What are ye doin' alone in the woods te begin with?" He replaced his sword in the scabbard at his waist.

"I . . . was using a bush," she said for lack of anything else coming to mind.

"Then ye better go on back te yer clan afore those English curs cause ye any more trouble."

"I dinna think they will."

He looked surprised by her comment as he walked up to her. "Why would ye think a thing like thet?"

"Because . . . ye scared them away. And I ken I'm safe now thet I'm with ye."

He seemed to like that answer, as the corners of his mouth turned upward into a smile of satisfaction. She knew that Highlanders thought highly of themselves, and a few compliments would get her far.

"Me name is Aidan. Aidan MacKeefe," he said. His tawny brown eyes studied her, and she saw a kindness within them. His blond hair hung down to his shoulders, lifting in the slight summer breeze, making him look like some sort of pagan god. Stubble shadowed his face in a slight mustache and beard, adding to the ruggedness of his composure. He wore a white leine, long tunic down to his knees, with the lacings untied, showing his sturdy chest. His plaid was wrapped around him and thrown over one shoulder. He seemed to have large muscles, and looked to be very strong. She liked that. She hadn't been so close to a handsome man . . . ever.

"Are ye a Highlander?" she asked, surveying his rugged looks. She was from the Lowlands, and knew that Highlanders were said to be barbaric and mad.

"I am," he said, and before she could say anything more, a squirrel dropped down from the tree above and landed on his shoulder. She screamed and jumped back, but he didn't even flinch. He reached out for the animal, and it scurried from one of his arms to the other before settling on his back, peering over the top with wide eyes.

"There's – a squirrel on yer back," she said, just in case he hadn't noticed.

"I ken," he said, his eyes never leaving her for a moment. "Thet's me pet, Reid."

Now she knew he was one of those crazy Highlanders she'd

heard about. This point proved it. "How nice," she said and forced a smile.

"So are ye goin' te tell me yer name, me bonnie cailin?"

"I'm Effie," she said, finding herself getting lost within the swirling depths of his eyes. His perusal of her drew her in, making her feel excited. He was not only ruggedly handsome, but he was also looking at her as if her presence excited him as well. She'd never felt anything like this in her life.

Tasgall stepped through the trees making his presence known just then, and ruining her magical moment. "She is Effie MacDuff and she is here with me," he said, and shot her a sickening smirk.

"Ye are a MacDuff?" Aidan asked in surprise.

"Aye, I am Effie MacDuff," she admitted, and smiled, hoping the MacKeefes and the MacDuffs weren't in the midst of some kind of feud.

"And who are you?" he asked, surveying Tasgall from head to toe.

"I'm Tasgall. I am a gypsy," he said. "Effie and I are the last ones left o' our little family, as the English have attacked and killed off the rest jest the other day."

"A gypsy?" He looked confused. "But I thought the lassie was a MacDuff." His hand went to the hilt of his sword, and Effie knew he didn't trust them.

"It's true," she said, stepping in between them. "Me mathair was once a MacDuff but broke away from the clan. I was raised as a gypsy, a traveler, jest wandering the land."

"I dinna understand," he said, still eyeing up Tasgall cautiously. Effie could see she would never get any information out of any Scot if Tasgall decided to tag along. He had a face that could not be trusted, and his eyes were shifty. He also wore raggedy clothes. No one trusted a gypsy in the first place, and it was going to be hard enough to gather information now that the Highlander knew she was a gypsy as well. The idiot, Tasgall, may have very well just ruined her chance to save her sister.

"Me throat is parched," she said, clearing her throat. "Aidan MacKeefe, would ye mind takin' me somewhere so I can get somethin' te drink?"

"I kennawhat ye like te drink, but Callum MacKeefe is the owner o' the Horn and Hoof pub and he brews a mean mountain magic," Aidan told her.

She had no idea what he was talking about, but he was offering to take her to a pub, and she was sure there'd be lots of loose tongues in there. Hopefully she could gather the information she needed to help save her sister.

"Thet sounds good te me," said Tasgall.

Effie just scowled at him. "Dinna ye need te go fetch our supplies so we have somethin' te eat tonight?"

When Aidan turned to look at the man, Effie motioned with her head for him to leave them alone.

"I'll meet ye at the pub in a wee bit then," Tasgall said, nodding and hurrying away.

"Well then," she said, releasing a deep breath and brushing the leaves and dirt from her clothes, "shall we go and get us some o' thet mountain magic?" She grabbed onto Aidan's arm, and almost laughed when he jolted in surprise.

"All right," he said. "Let us go get te ken each other better."

He led her to the pub, and once inside, she saw a bunch of rowdy Scots gathered around a table hooting and hollering as two of the men arm-wrestled. Coins hit the table as people placed their bets, and the roar in the room grew.

"What's goin' on?" she asked.

"Oh, thet's jest me friends foolin' around, havin' had too much te drink as usual."

She watched a dark-haired man with two different colored eyes collecting the bets as a big, ugly old Scot with rotten teeth arm-wrestled another very handsome Scot with dark hair and bulging muscles. The latter won the competition and jumped up and shook a fist in the air in triumph. Then the pub keeper passed out drinks for everyone. Aidan grabbed one and downed it in one move, then took another off the server's tray and handed it to her.

"Try it," he said. "It's mountain magic. But until ye're used te it, ye'd –"

She downed it the way he had, and plunked the drinking vessel back down atop the server's tray. Then she felt it - fire raging like a hot poker in her throat, blazing a trail down her chest all the way to her stomach.

"- better jest take a sip," he added, a little too late.

She clutched her throat and gasped for breath, bending over, feeling like she was going to die.

"Are ye all right, lassie?" he asked, patting her on the back. His squirrel scampered off his shoulder and down her arm to the drink board, scaring her out of her wits. She jerked upward quickly and ended up falling into his arms.

The heat of his embrace engulfed her as his arms wrapped around her in a protective manner. His strength was evident, and she felt more protected than she'd ever felt in her entire life. She was short, and he was tall, and her head rested against the bare skin of his chest peeking out from his untied leine.

"I tried te warn ye," he told her with a smile.

"I'm fine," she gasped out in a breathy voice. "Jest fine." Her head dizzied and she held onto him as her body swayed.

"Aidan, ye take on Ian now, as he's been undefeated all night," shouted out the man with two different colored eyes.

AIDAN WAS GOING to object to the challenge, until Effie urged him on.

"Come on, do it," she said.

He looked down to her, and noticed the dazed look in her eyes from the potent whisky.

"I dinna think so," he said, which only earned him shouts from the drunken crowd.

"What's the matter, afeard te let me see those big, bad muscles?" Effie snaked her hand under his leine and squeezed the top of his arm. "I like the feel of it," she said with a big smile. Aidan knew it was the whisky talking, but he never turned down a chance to impress a bonnie lassie. If he played his cards right, he may just have this one in his bed by tonight.

"All right," he said, sitting down and facing Ian.

"Who's the lassie ye picked up?" asked Ian, clasping hands with him as Onyx started counting down for them to start.

"Her name is Effie."

"If she's a hoor, mayhap ye'll share her when ye're done?"

Effie leaned up against the back of him, and he could tell that she was having a hard time standing.

"She's no' a hoor," he said, hoping he was right, because he rather liked her, and she was very pretty. He also didn't want to share her – especially with Ian who had a charming way with women that he knew he could never match.

"Three . . . two . . . one . . . go!" shouted Onyx, letting loose of their hands.

It was an even challenge, neither of them being able to move the other's hand, and then Ian looked up and winked at Effie.

"Stop thet," warned Aidan.

"Greetin's, lassie," Ian said to her. "Me name is Ian, and me friend here is Dagger," he said nodding toward Onyx. "Will ye come and hang on me next the way ye're clingin' te Aidan?"

"I've had enough." Aidan slammed Ian's hand to the table in anger, and Onyx declared him the winner.

"Quit bein' so sore," said Ian, laughing. "I was only tryin' te see if the lassie would consider a threesome with us later."

That did it. Aidan lunged over the table, taking his friend to the ground. They rolled around on the floor until Ian got Aidan in one of his headlocks once again.

"What did ye do thet fer?" asked Ian.

"I dinna like what ye said about the lassie."

"Och, I thought ye liked threesomes," Ian said in his defense.

"No' with another man," growled Aidan. "And no one is havin' a threesome with Effie."

"What's the matter with ye, Aidan?" Onyx walked up to them.

"I willna let Ian steal this one," said Aidan. "She's mine, I tell ye, so back off."

He didn't normally act so possessive over a girl he'd just met, and normally didn't mind sharing. However, something about this one touched a place in his heart. He felt like he knew her from somewhere, as she seemed familiar, but he just couldn't place her. He also felt as if he needed to protect her. Not understanding why he was feeling this way, the only thing that was clear was that he didn't want Ian anywhere near her.

"Aidan, ye picked yerself a feisty one this time," said Onyx.

"What do ye mean?" he said from under Ian's arm.

"Dinna look now, but she's arm-wrestling one o' the pub's hoors."

"She's what?" Aidan pushed out from under Ian's arm, and they both joined Onyx in standing there with their mouths gaping open as Effie sat in the same spot the men just vacated, with her sleeve rolled up, and arm-wrestling one of the pub's whores.

Coins flew in all directions, and the men in the pub made a big ruckus, falling over each other as they ran to the table where the women competed.

"Effie, what're ye doin'?" asked Aidan, walking up behind her, pushing a few men to the side in the process.

"I think thet mountain magic has gotten me bluid flowin'," she said with a flushed face and a very big smile. "I'm feelin' lucky, I tell ye. I'm goin' te win."

Then in one slam to the table, Effie brought the whore's arm down, and they declared her the winner. She jumped atop the chair and raised her hands above her head in triumph. Aidan stepped next to her just as she lost her balance and fell. He caught her, and when he did, her arm with the rolled up sleeve was right in front of his face. His eyes opened wide as his gaze settled on a strawberry birthmark on the inside of her forearm. It looked like a skull. Now he knew exactly why he felt as if he knew her. He did.

"Ye are the lassie from me dream," he said aloud.

"What dream?" she asked with a giggle.

"The dream I had when I slept on the Stone o' Scone."

"The what?" she asked.

"Ye ken. The Stone o' Destiny."

"The Stone o' Destiny?" Her eyes widened and she stopped laughing. "Ye ken where it is?"

"O' course I do," said Aidan. "And now I ken why ye seemed so familiar. Ye are the lassie from me dream. Me Scottish angel."

CHAPTER 4

MadMan MacKeefe Series

"Aidan, ye didna really jest say thet to a stranger?" Ian stood in front of Aidan with his arms crossed.

"This is Effie," he said, placing her on her feet. "She is a MacDuff, so we can trust her. After all, the MacDuffs guarded the stone a few years ago, isna thet right?" he asked Effie.

"Oh. . . . I suppose thet's right," she agreed, and giggled.

"Excuse me, me bonnie cailin, but we need te steal Aidan fer a moment." Ian dragged Aidan away from her with a grip on his leine, and Onyx followed as they hauled him to a darkened corner.

"Get yer bluidy hands off me afore I break yer wrist," Aidan warned him.

Ian let go and just shook his head. "Ye jest told a perfect stranger about the stone. What were ye thinkin'?"

"Aye," agreed Aidan, looking in her direction and smiling. "She is perfect, I agree."

"We dinna ken her at all," said Onyx. "Fer all we ken she could be some sort o' spy and workin' fer the English."

"Och, ye two worry too much." He looked at them when he spoke now. "She is no' goin' te tell anyone."

"How can ye be so sure?" asked Onyx.

Aidan looked over to see the girl now trying to balance a wooden cup on her head and walk a straight line atop the table at the same time. The Scots in the pub were well in their cups and coaxing her forward.

"Because, she is no' thet kind o' lassie. I saw her in me dream. I think I am supposed te help keep her safe."

"Ye think thet about any bonnie cailin," scowled Onyx.

"Aye," agreed Ian. "And dinna ferget ye also saw English soldiers in the dream too."

"But I saved her from two English bastards tryin' te couple with her against her will. I am sure thet's what the dream meant."

"What about the tail?" asked Onyx. "Ye, yerself, pointed out the old sayin' thet our enemies have tails."

"Blethers, ye two were the ones who scoffed at me dream in the first place. Ye also reminded me thet the tail was naught but me squirrel sleepin' on me chest. So dinna fash yerself, I am sure she will keep our secret."

"I hope ye're right," said Onyx. "Because if she runs back and tells anyone, the Chieftain will have our heids. No' te mention, the MacKeefes will ne'er be trusted again, especially as guardians o' the stone."

"Who is she here with, anyway?" asked Ian.

"She says she's a gypsy and the English killed off her traveling companions. She was with only one man, but I dinna ken where he went."

"Then ye'd better keep an eye on her and make sure she hauds her wheesht," said Onyx. "After all, she seems like she could have a loose tongue right now, since she obviously canna hold her whisky."

"I'll make sure she disna leave me side tonight," Aidan assured them. "After all, I wouldna want te lose me dream angel."

"Well, if she starts sproutin' a tail, be sure te tell us," said Ian very seriously. Then he looked at Aidan and just smiled.

Aidan swung at him, but Ian ducked, and Onyx took the brunt of his fist to the face instead. In a matter of seconds, the three of them were in a brawl, and the drunkards in the pub joined in, breaking chairs and pouring drinks over each other's heads.

EFFIE LOOKED up at the sound of the commotion, her quick movement causing the wooden cup to fall from her head to the floor. When she lowered herself from the table to get it, a bottle whizzing through the air just missed her and hit the drink board, smashing into pieces. She stood up straight and almost fell over from still not being stable from the whisky. That's when Aidan appeared through the crowd and grabbed her hand and pulled her toward the door.

"Stop it, all o' ye," called the pub keeper. "Ye madmen are goin' te pay fer this, I swear."

"Fast, we need te get goin'," Aidan told her.

"I just got here," she said, almost tripping over a broken chair as Aidan pulled her toward the door. "Where are we goin'?"

"Anywhere away from here," he said, pulling her out into the sunlight and quickly closing the door. The door to the pub burst open behind them, and she looked over her shoulder to see Ian and Onyx being dragged out by their ears by the feeble old pub keeper.

"Are yer friends goin' te be alright?" she asked.

"Och, lassie. Me and me friends have been in worse situations than this afore."

He pulled her to the stables and into a stall, and started to saddle a horse.

"Are ye takin' me somewhere, Aidan?"

"Aye. I'm takin' ye somewhere fer the night where ye can sober up before ye do anything doitit."

"Me do somethin' doitit?" she asked, finding humor in the situation. "I am no' the one who started the brawl in the pub."

"Well, it's no' the first time me and me friends have been thrown out o' the Horn and Hoof by old Callum MacKeefe, and it willna be the last time, I promise."

"Ye make me smile," she said, when he turned to help her atop the horse.

"I'm glad someone finds me amusin' tonight." He put his hands on her waist to lift her up, and Effie found herself enjoying the intimacy of it. She could smell the Highland air in his hair and the whisky on his breath. Or mayhap that was her, she wasn't sure.

"I ne'er thanked ye fer savin' me from those English curs," she said, and before he could respond, she reached over and kissed him on the mouth. He pulled back and looked at her in shock, and then to her surprise, he put his hand at the back of her head and dipped down for another kiss.

Effie was lost in the sensual act, knowing she'd lost her mind, and no longer caring. She'd never felt this way from a kiss before, but then again, the only kisses she'd ever gotten in her life we from gypsy men, not strong, handsome Highland warriors.

His lips were soft and pleasurable, as he claimed her in a lover's embrace. There was nothing shy about his kiss. She could tell by the way his tongue entered her mouth that he was very experienced with the lassies.

Her head dizzied and she didn't know if it was from the kiss or the whisky. Either way, she liked it, and wrapped her arms around Aidan's neck, pulling herself closer. When she tried to repeat the action, wanting more, he just lifted her up and hoisted her into the saddle.

"We need te get movin'," he told her. "There'll be time fer thet later."

"I'll be lookin' forward te it," she answered boldly.

He climbed up behind her, reaching around her to grab the reins and direct the horse from the stall, and she felt like a caterpillar in a cocoon, enclosed in his warm embrace. Leaning back against him, she once again felt safe in his arms. She hoped what he said was true, as she really wanted another kiss from the madman sitting behind her.

Thinking he would head in the opposite direction of the pub where the fighting was still going on, she was surprised when instead he rode right up to the door and hopped off the horse.

"What are ye doin'?" she asked. "Ye're mad if ye plan on goin' back in there right now."

"Aye, some people say thet."

"Let's jest keep goin'."

"I canna jest leave me friends," he said, and headed for Ian and Onyx who were standing outside the pub.

"Dagger," said Aidan, "I am sorry fer hittin' ye in the jaw."

"Dinna worry about it." Onyx rubbed his face. "But if I dinna go back te me wife in one piece ye may have te worry about her comin' after ye instead. After all, a bairned lassie has many moods thet I'll ne'er understand."

"Why is *she* on yer horse?" asked Ian, looking over to Effie who was smoothing down her hair, and almost lost her balance and grabbed quickly for the saddle horn.

"Because I canna jest leave her here."

"Because she's yer angel?" Ian scowled at her.

"Nay. Because she had one wee dram o' mountain magic and canna stand straight. No' te mention, I was thinkin' o' what ye two said, and I need te make sure she willna wag her tongue about the stone."

"I thought ye said ye trusted her," said Onyx.

"I do."

"So takin' her with ye is just an excuse te bed her?" asked Ian. "After all, we ken yer ways with the lassies."

"Me ways are no different than yers, Ian," he said with a shake of his head. "But thet's no' why." Aidan looked over to Effie and she smiled and waved slightly. He waggled his fingers in the air and smiled back.

"Aye, we can see thet." Onyx rolled his eyes.

"Nay, really," said Aidan. "It's because I willna leave her alone after those English bastards tried te defile her earlier."

"Well, where's the gypsy man ye said was with her?" asked Ian. "Surely, he can take care o' her."

"I dinna ken, and I dinna care. He had shifty eyes and I'd rather no' see him again tonight, nor do I feel he can protect her. Now I'm goin' inside the pub te find Reid and then I'm headin' back to camp."

"Ye canna go in there right now," said Ian. "Old Callum is madder than a hornet at all the damage thet's been done. He's blamin' us ye realize."

"Thet's right," said Onyx. "And ye ken the MacKeefes are all stayin' at the fair fer at least the rest o' the week."

"I'll go back and guard the stone and give Renard and Niall a chance te come te the fair, then," said Aidan.

"Then we'll go with ye," said Onyx, and Ian nodded.

"Guid, now give me the money ye won from the arm-wrestlin'," Aidan said, looking at Onyx.

"I kennawhat ye mean."

"Hand it o'er," said Aidan, holding out his palm.

"I need the extra coin. After all, I have a bairn comin' soon." Onyx did not want to give it up.

"If we dinna pay fer the damages, ye ken our chieftain will have us shovelin' jobby from the stables fer the next month."

"He's right," said Ian. "With Callum bein' Storm's grandda and all, we willna have a moment's peace back at camp until we've made guid fer the loss."

"Fine. Take it," said Onyx, pulling the pouch of coins from his waist and shoving it into Aidan's hands.

"Now, go get yer horses and let's head out o' here before any o' the Scots inside decide they want another match at tryin' te win back their coins." Aidan turned on his heel, and headed into the pub.

EFFIE WAITED from atop the horse, watching as a pouch of coins was exchanged and Aidan headed inside the pub. His friends hurried toward the stable.

"What did ye find out?" came a voice from the ground.

She looked down to see Tasgall standing there. Not the person she wanted to see right now, or ever.

"Dinna talk so loud," she said, looking back toward the pub, hoping no one had heard them. "I lucked out. The Scot thet saved me, kens where the stone is."

"Lord Ralston will be happy te hear about it," said Tasgall. "Well, where is it?"

"I dinna ken yet, but I'm guessin' it's back at their camp since he said somethin' about sleepin' on it. Go report te Lord Ralston and then ask around where te find the MacKeefe camp, and follow with the soldiers."

"It'll take several days te do thet, and I dinna even have a horse."

"Then go find the bluidy curs thet tried te accost me and get them te give ye a ride. I'm sure they're lurkin' around here somewhere. Now go back and tell that bluidy bastard, Lord Ralston, thet I'll get him the information he needs, but if he harms me sister in any way, I'll make sure he ne'er gets his hand on the stone. Do ye understand?"

"I canna let ye outta me sight. Thet was orders from Lord Ralston himself."

"Why no'? Ye ken I willna run. Me sister's life means more te me than anythin'. I am goin' te try te get the Scot te show me the stone. Now do as I say and be gone from me sight, as I dinna want such a filthy, traitorous liar in me presence."

"Ye are about to become no better than me, so I wouldna

point fingers if I were ye. All right then, I'll go. But if ye are tryin' te trick me, I assure ye yer sister will no' live te see ye again, so dinna cross us. Do ye understand me?"

"If I wasna so dizzy from the whisky, I'd jump off this horse and bury yer face in the ground jest fer threatenin' me. Now go," she said, seeing Aidan coming out of the pub. "I dinna want him te see us talkin'."

Tasgall had no sooner stepped away from the horse than Aidan was mounted behind her with his squirrel on his shoulder.

"Isna thet the gypsy man ye came with?" he asked.

Too late. He saw them talking. She just hoped he hadn't heard their conversation.

"Aye," she said.

"Where is he goin'?"

"Tasgall has decided te go find a new band o' gypsies fer us te live with, or mayhap a horse and supplies anyway. He said he'll catch up te me later."

"Was he yer lover?"

The thought of this almost caused her to retch. "Dinna make me laugh," she said. "If Tasgall e'er tried te touch me, I'd have severed his head from his body with me dirk."

"Really? I find thet interestin' since ye dinna seem te carry any weapons."

"The English guards took them from me," she said, thinking quickly. "However, I plan on replacin' me weapons soon."

"With what?"

"What do ye mean?"

"I dinna see a sporran o' coins at yer waist, and ye said ye just lost e'erythin' when the English attacked yer camp. Ye dinna plan te hoor yerself out te get them, do ye?"

"If thet's what ye think o' me, Aidan MacKeefe, then let me off this horse right now, as I'll no' be comin' te yer camp with ye after all."

"Who said we were goin' to me camp?"

"Well . . . I jest assumed ye would want te get a good rest. That ye'd want te sleep on thet stone thet gives ye guid dreams."

"I ne'er said the dreams were guid."

"Nay? I thought ye said I was in yer dream." She turned to look at him and his lips were so close to hers that she wondered if he was going to kiss her again. She really wanted him to, but to her disappointment, he just turned his head and looked the other way.

"Ye were in me dream, but if it was guid or no' is yet te be seen."

Effie wasn't sure what that meant, but liked the fact that she was in his dreams, and also the fact he'd called her his dream angel.

"So do ye have somewhere te stay, Effie?" he asked her.

"Nay," she admitted. "I am homeless and have no friends."

"Couldna ye go back te the MacDuffs?"

"I dinna ken them. I told ye me mathair wasna a part o' the clan, though she had the bloodright te be there. I dinna think they would want me, though."

"Then ye'll come with me te the MacKeefe camp until we can find ye a place te stay. I willna leave ye alone, as the English soldiers might come back and try te cause ye trouble again."

"I'd like te come with ye," she said, as they rode up to meet Aidan's friends. She smiled to herself thinking how easy this was going to be. She'd collect the information of where the stone was, then direct her sister's captors right to it when they arrived. Aye, before she knew it, Coira would be free and they'd head overseas or somewhere to start a new life – just the two of them together.

CHAPTER 5

*M*aking it back to the MacKeefe camp couldn't be done in a day, so Aidan decided they'd stop and camp for the night at the north edge of Loch Lomond. The sun was just setting. The day had been hot, and they were all weary, and Aidan wanted nothing more than to wash off the dust from his travels, taking a swim in the water.

After the horses were taken care of, and the supplies unloaded that they'd picked up at the trade fair, Aidan continued to set up camp by tending to a fire.

"We're goin' up te the bluff te take a swim," said Onyx. "Did ye want te come with us, Aidan?"

He wanted it more than anything, but didn't want to leave the girl unattended.

"Nay, I'll hunt something fer us te eat," he said.

"Go ahead, join them," said Effie. "Just give me that bow and arrows you brought from the fair and I'll take care of huntin' fer our dinner."

"Mayhap ye'd better stay after all," said Ian, giving him a look that Aidan knew meant he didn't trust the lassie.

The two took off up the cliff, and Aidan just added more

kindling to the fire. His squirrel rooted around in the dirt, looking for food.

"I ken ye want te go with them," Effie said. "Just go."

"Nay, I dinna want te leave ye alone."

"I'm a gypsy, I live off the land. We dinna see anyone followin' us, so I'll be fine."

He just looked back down to the fire and shook his head. He was torn, and though he trusted that she wouldn't leave, he was trying to proceed with caution, as his friends had warned him to do. Aidan always was the most trusting one of the three of them, and had on more than one occasion been burned because of it.

"I dinna ken if it's a guid idea."

"Oh. Ye dinna trust me, jest like yer friends."

He looked over to her and saw the disappointment on her face. He didn't want to make her feel this way, he only wanted to please her. She was the most beautiful lassie he'd ever met, and he loved her fearlessness. He got to his feet and went over to the supplies and pulled out a bow and arrows.

"Ye can use these," he said. "I willna be gone long. Dinna go too far from the camp as once ye get away from the fire, ye may encounter a wildcat or a wolf."

"I can protect meself," she said.

"Aye. I saw how well ye did thet with those English guards."

"If I'd had a weapon, they'd be deid right now."

"I'm no' so sure, lassie. Now jest do me a favor and dinna shoot any squirrels, as I dinna want me pet killed. Reid, go on up and hide in a tree," he said over his shoulder. The little red squirrel scampered up a tree and away from them.

EFFIE WATCHED in amazement as the man's squirrel seemed to understand him, and on command disappeared into the trees.

"Thet is a strange pet fer anyone te have," she said, shaking her head.

"No' as strange as Onyx's pet," Aidan mumbled, walking away.

"What does he have? A pine marten or somethin'?" she called after him.

"Nothin' thet tame, I assure ye. Now jest call out if ye need me, as I won't be far. And if ye think ye'er goin' te catch somethin' te eat, ye'd better hurry, as it's startin' te get dark."

She watched him disappear into the thicket, thinking there must be some sort of pond they were going to swim in up on the cliffs. She had no idea why they just didn't swim in the lake. She'd never understand these men.

Effie picked up her bow and arrows and used her senses to tell her where she might find prey. It wasn't going to be that easy once it got dark, Aidan was right. The sun was starting to set now, so she'd have to hurry.

She didn't have to hunt long before she spotted and took down a carrion crow that was irritating her with its squawking. She also managed to shoot a red grouse as well, just before it got dark. The men would surely be impressed with her ability to use a weapon and hunt. Not too many women could do what she'd just done and in such a short amount of time. They would eat well tonight. It might not be a deer, but it was still a meal.

Planning on heading back to camp, the lake looked inviting, so she decided to stay. She was hot and felt so dirty, not only from the road but from being locked in a cage and also pawed by the English guards.

Effie looked around but didn't see the men, and figured she had time for a quick dip before she headed back. Throwing down the dead birds at the edge of the lake, she quickly removed her clothes and slipped into the water. That's when she heard shouts – and they were coming from up at the top of the cliff.

As darkness started to cover the land, she looked upward to see three naked men diving off a cliff into the waters below – not far from where she was. They were laughing, shouting, and having fun. She knew immediately it was Aidan and his friends.

"What in the clootie's name are they doin'?" she asked aloud. It was dangerous enough to dive off a cliff during the day, but to do so when it was nighttime was only something a madman would attempt.

She decided to get dressed and head back and start the meal, but when she stepped naked from the water, she was greeted by a low growl. Some kind of wild animal, possibly a wolf or a hound was there on the shore. Not able to see it well in the dark, all she could really tell was that is was very large. It had its head lowered as it moved into the moonlight, enabling her to see it better now. Long legs led to scraggly grayish hair on the animal, the hair so long and matted that she could barely see its eyes. It was moving quickly toward the dead birds. When it saw her, it looked up and showed its teeth, then changed its direction. The thing looked gaunt and possibly injured, as it had dried blood on its fur and limped when it came toward her.

She didn't know what to do. Her clothes as well as her weapon were on the other side of the animal. She'd never be able to get to them before it attacked her. She should have backed up and slid back into the water for safety, but if so, she knew the animal would probably steal both of her birds. She couldn't have that. She was hungrier than hell since Lord Ralston hadn't fed her much. Besides, she wanted Aidan to like her, and she wanted to impress him with what she'd caught for dinner.

So instead of walking away from the animal, she shouted at it, waving her arms in the air, and daringly moved forward.

* * *

AIDAN WAS ALREADY SWIMMING, making his way toward shore when he heard Effie shouting. He looked through the darkness and spotted her on the shore just a short distance from them.

"Haud yer wheesht," he called out to his friends. "I think Effie is in trouble."

Onyx and Ian stopped their splashing and looked toward the shore as well.

"Is she naked?" asked Ian, squinting his eyes, trying to see through the darkness.

"Aye, I think so," said Aidan. "But what is she doin'?" Then he saw the animal coming toward her, and instead of backing away, the fool girl was going straight for it. "She's bein' attacked!" He swam full force through the water with his friends right behind him. He made it to the shore first, being the best swimmer of the three of them, and ran down the water's edge as fast as he could to save Effie.

EFFIE MADE her way closer to the dead birds on the ground, planning on grabbing at least one of them before the wild animal stole them, when out of nowhere, Aidan darted out from the darkness, hitting her like a stone wall, taking her down with him into the water. The water splashed over her head and she sputtered for breath.

"What the hell are ye doin'?" she shouted, now down in the water with Aidan's body – his naked body - covering hers.

"I'll protect ye, lassie. Jest stay here." He jumped to his feet and headed toward the animal, taking it down to the ground as well. He had no weapons on him, no clothes, no anything, but wrestled with it as if he were doing naught but arm-wresting another Scot at the pub.

Then his friends darted out of the shadows as well, both of them naked, too. She just sat there in the water with her mouth open, as the moonlight spilled over their bodies. Each of them just as fit as the next, and she could only think this was one of her lusty dreams. No woman she knew would ever be witnessing what she was seeing in front of her very eyes.

The animal growled and snapped at Aidan, and twisted, kicking up its legs as Aidan tried to hold it down.

"Aidan, put it in a headlock," shouted Ian.

"I'm no guid at headlocks the way ye are, Ian. And this is no' a person, it's an animal with sharp claws and even sharper teeth."

"Jest let it go," called out Onyx, coming toward the animal with a big stick in his hand. "I'll get it."

"Nay, I got it," Aidan called back, and Effie thought it was for her benefit that he refused to let it go. Then he did something that both surprised and amused her at the same time. He leaned over, his long, blond hair falling over his face, and he . . . bit the animal on the ear.

The animal whimpered, and he let it go. Then he got to his feet with his arms spread out wide. His friends were doing the same. Aidan's bare doup was facing her now, and she realized he had muscles everywhere on his body, and not a bit of fat. He was the perfect image of a woman's fantasy man. His friends may have been as mesmerizing, but since her eyes were fastened on Aidan, she really wouldn't know.

The chattering of a squirrel was heard and Effie saw Aidan's pet, Reid, making its way toward him over the ground.

"Go away, Reid," shouted Aidan. "Shoo, afore ye are this beast's dinner."

To her horror, the animal lunged at the squirrel. It may have caught the squirrel if Ian hadn't picked up the dead grouse and thrown it as a distraction. The animal stopped, its head low, its eyes focusing on Ian. She thought for a moment it was going to attack him, but instead, it grabbed the dead bird and quickly limped away.

That angered Effie, as there went half their dinner. So, not caring that she was naked, she got up out of the water and stormed to the shore.

"What did you do thet fer?" she shouted at the men.

AIDAN TURNED AROUND to see Effie standing there in the moonlight, naked, and looking like a goddess of the sea. Her small form didn't matter, as she made herself look intimidating with a scowl on her face and her hands on her hips. Her red locks were wet and the strands stuck to her chest, sending water droplets running in rivulets over her firm, perky breasts. Her nipples were cold and taut, and the nest of red hair between her firm and shapely thighs was just as red as that on her head.

All three men just stood there staring with their jaws dropped open, and then Aidan realized that she was seeing his friends naked as well. He didn't like any of this. He took a step to block her, and looked over to his friends.

"Go get our clothes, and we'll meet ye back at the camp."

"O' course," said Onyx, turning to leave. But when Ian was still standing there, he reached over and grabbed his arm. "Come on, Ian, this one isna yers."

Aidan didn't turn back around until they were gone. When he did, he felt the sharp sting of a slap to his face.

"What was thet fer?" he asked, his hand going to his cheek.

"Fer givin' away our dinner." Effie stormed over to the dead crow that was being inspected by Reid. The squirrel scolded her and scampered away as she picked up the bird by the feet. "I caught this as well as a grouse, but now thanks to ye three, thet wolf is goin' te be eatin' better than us tonight."

"Thet was no wolf, believe me. It looked te me like a wolfhound though, and I think it was wounded."

"Whate'er it was, it has our dinner."

"Well, ye're welcome thet I saved yer life twice in one day," he said. "And I wasna the one who gave the grouse te the hound, if I must remind ye. That was Ian."

"Ye three are fools!" She stormed over to her clothes and started to don them. Aidan would have loved to look at her perfect, alluring body longer, but she quickly hid it from his sight.

"Why do ye say thet, lassie?"

"Because ye're standing there naked, arena ye?"

"So were ye."

"But I wasna divin' off the cliffs in the dark. Ye coulda killed yerself."

"Nay. We do it all the time."

"In the dark?" She was fully clothed now and pulled on her shoes as she spoke.

"It's more o' a challenge in the dark. How do ye think we earned our titles o' being madmen?"

She turned to him then, and her eyes scanned down his body. Her perusal caused him to become excited, and he felt his manhood growing quickly.

"Like what ye see?" Aidan smiled. "Because if ye do, we can do somethin' about it."

"Ye are no better than those English curs who tried te take me in the forest."

"What?" he asked, totally confused. "Effie, I am askin', no' takin' like they were." He held up his hands in a mock form of surrender.

"Well, dinna ask me again, fer I'm no' interested." She picked up the crow and headed through the dark forest, making her way to camp. Hopefully, Aidan believed her statement of not wanting him, because she wanted him badly but didn't want him to know it. She was trying her hardest not to fall for him, because she knew in a matter of time she was going to have to betray not only him but her country as well. The last thing she wanted to do was to break a heart. Especially if it was her own.

CHAPTER 6

*T*he next morning, Aidan busied himself breaking down camp and preparing the horses rather than have to talk to Effie. She finally gave up trying to talk to him, and headed down to the lake a while ago. After the way she made all three of them feel so guilty, they'd all given up their portion of the crow last night in order for her to eat.

"I'm starvin'" grumbled Ian, coming to join him by the horses.

"Well, mayhap ye shoulda thought o' thet before ye went and gave our dinner te the hound," Aidan pointed out.

"The poor thing looked so skinny and hungry," said Ian. "Did ye see the way it limped and had blood on its fur? It was hurt. Mayhap attacked by wolves. With the shape it was in, it probably didna even make it through the night."

"Jest another reason why ye shouldna have fed it." Aidan secured the travel bags to the horses. The bags were filled with supplies from the fair.

"Mayhap we can find the hound's deid body and eat it te break the fast," said Onyx, rubbing a weary hand over his face and coming to join them.

"Dinna say thet!" Ian seemed disturbed by the suggestion. "I couldna eat thet poor animal, no' after seeing thet sad look in its eyes."

"Well, ye had no qualms about wantin' te eat me squirrel when we first found it." Aidan looked around, realizing he hadn't seen his squirrel since it fell asleep on his chest by the fire last night. "Where is Reid anyway? We're almost ready te go."

"Guid mornin'," came Effie's cheerful voice as she made her way up from the lake and toward them, with a string of dead fish in her hand and Aidan's squirrel on her shoulder. Aidan couldn't believe his eyes.

"How many fish have ye got there?" asked Ian eagerly, his eyes fastened to his next meal.

"Forget the fish, what are ye doin' with me squirrel on yer shoulder?" Aidan reached out and took his pet back from her and placed it on the ground.

"Well, Reid seems te like me," she said. "And Ian, I got up early te fish in the loch. Would ye care fer a bite te eat afore we leave?"

"Aye," said Ian, quickly reaching out for the fish.

"Nay!" Aidan stepped in front of him and took the fish from Effie. "We'll take these back te camp and share them with the boys who stayed behind te guard the stone." He turned and started tying them to the side of the horse.

"I shoulda ate yer damn squirrel," mumbled Ian, making his way to put out the fire.

"Too bad the supplies we are bringin' back from the fair arena food," grumbled Onyx, going to his horse.

"So . . . is this stone thet the boys are guardin', the Stone o' Destiny, by any chance?" asked Effie.

"Dinna worry about it." Aidan was in no mood for talking, nor to give her any information she wanted after she'd rejected him last night. He held out his hands to help her get atop the horse. "Let's go."

She let him help her atop the horse, and he wondered what happened to the grouchy girl from last night who'd sat there glaring at him and his friends and hadn't even bothered to thank them for helping her with the hound.

He pulled himself atop the horse, settling in behind her, and they headed toward MacKeefe territory. With any luck they'd be there by this afternoon, and he'd be able to take a nap on his dream stone since he'd laid awake all night, watching for the hound to come back, determined to guard his angel even if she said she didn't want him.

This, for some odd reason, only made Aidan want her even more.

EFFIE KNEW she'd been harsh with Aidan last night, as well as his friends. She felt the tension between them all, and that's why she'd woken up early and decided to fish. She wanted to make amends between them. Aidan's feelings were obviously hurt when she told him she didn't want him last night. Still, he couldn't deny the fact he'd wanted her, because his body didn't lie. She'd seen his immense desire to lay with her, and actually that was another reason why she'd denied him.

He scared her - and she didn't scare easily. She'd had a hard life, and even with all her trials and tribulations, she'd always managed to keep her head about her. With Aidan, things were different. She couldn't stop thinking of the kiss they'd shared and the way he'd risked his life twice now to save her.

She supposed she was so mean to him because she didn't feel as if she deserved his acts of kindness. He'd even convinced his friends to give their portion of the crow last night to her. She'd gladly eaten it, even though she hated eating crow. She'd been so hungry after not having really eaten in the last few days, that she accepted the offer.

Wanting more than anything to eat the fish this morning, she ended up deciding she wasn't going to fight with Aidan if he said they needed to be on their way. It was probably better that they just get to camp as fast as possible and get this all over with. She'd been so upset thinking about her sister trapped in that English bastard's cage last night, that she didn't sleep a wink, even though she was dead tired.

Stifling a yawn, Effie ran a finger over the back of the squirrel now sitting on the horn of the saddle. The cute little thing had taken a liking to her for some reason.

"Reid likes ye," she heard Aidan say from behind her.

"Well, I like him, too," she said, not turning her head to talk. If she did, her face would be pressed up against Aidan's and she'd want to kiss him again. "So, tell me about yer dream stone," she said.

"What's there to tell?"

"Have ye had it long?"

"Why do ye keep askin' me about it?"

She froze. "I'm jest tryin' te make conversation." She hoped he didn't suspect what she was up to.

"I'd rather talk about yer family instead," he said.

"I told ye . . . I have no family." She truly wished to avoid this conversation. "Me faither died in battle and me mathair died givin' birth to me sister."

"So ye have a sister? What is her name?"

Damn, she didn't mean to tell him that. She had to be more careful. "Her name is Coira. But she . . . died," she lied. "When the English attacked our camp."

"I'm so sorry. I didna realize. I ken how hard this must be fer ye. If I can do anythin' te help ye ease the pain –"

"I dinna want te talk about it." Why did he have to be so nice? No one had ever been so nice to her in her entire life, and now that she found someone, she knew it wouldn't last. As soon as she did her dirty deed, Aidan would hate her forever.

They rode in silence for awhile, then she started wondering about him.

"Do ye have siblings?" she asked.

"I do," he said. "Me sister's name is Kyla. She is about yer age I'd guess."

"Is she married or have bairns?"

"Nay. She lives with the clan."

"I see. Are yer parents still alive?"

"Nay. I lost them both when I was verra young."

"In a battle?" she asked, curiously.

"Me faither died when he was thrown from a horse ten years ago, and me mathair died from fever when Kyla was only six. I am verra protective o' me wee sister and dinna like her bein' with any laddie."

"I am sorry fer yer loss as well," she said, "but Kyla is old enough te be married and have several bairns by now. Ye need te let loose with her, Aidan."

"I dinna ken. She will always be me wee sister, and I promised me mathair I'd watch o'er her."

Effie wanted to tell him that she and her sister were in a very similar situation. But she didn't. She didn't want him to know much about her, and nothing at all about her sister. It would only make things worse in the end.

"How old are ye, lass?"

"I am twenty summers . . . tomorrow," Effie answered.

"Tomorrow is yer birthday?"

"It is. But it no longer matters, as I have nothin' te celebrate."

"I'll make certain ye do," he said with promise to his voice.

"Nay, really. I dinna want anythin' done fer me. I dinna deserve it."

"How can ye say thet, Effie? Ye have lost yer whole family and e'erythin' te the English. I am goin' te make it up te ye. Especially since this will be yer first birthday without yer sister. I ken it'll be hard since ye've lost her just recently, but I will do me best te try te fill thet empty spot in yer heart."

She should have told him right then and there that her sister was still alive, but she couldn't. Lord Ralston's threat kept echoing in her brain. If she told anyone about her sister in the cage, the man would kill poor Coira. She couldn't take the chance. She had to keep it a secret for now, especially since she was so close to giving the bloody English what they wanted. Though it pained her to have to deceive Aidan and the MacKeefes, as well as turn traitor to her own country, she would do whatever it took to save her sister's life. Even if it meant gaining their trust and then deceiving a man who had been nothing but kind to her. Still, she'd never find someone like Aidan again in her life, and it pained her to be in this position.

He said he wanted to fill that empty spot in her heart, but little did he know that he already had.

CHAPTER 7

As soon as they got back to the MacKeefe camp, Renard and Niall came running out to join them. The MacKeefe camp had grown in the last few years, and now they had not only the cottage for the chieftain and his family, but also the hospice, as well as a dining cottage they used mostly in the winter, and nearly a dozen other cottages dotting the land that were for the other inhabitants. They were made of stone and had thatched roofs. There was a stable as well as a weaver's hut, and also a building that housed the homing pigeons that were kept by Wren for her brother, Madoc, who resided in Devonshire.

"Ye're back so soon?" asked Niall. The boy was the nephew of their chieftain, Storm MacKeefe, and was ten and six years of age. He wasn't very tall, but had a huge personality to make up for it.

"We are," he said, feeling Effie stir in his arms, as she'd fallen asleep for the last hour and he'd held her tightly as they rode, to ensure she didn't fall from the horse.

"Who is she?" asked Renard, Storm's red-haired son who was two years older than Niall. He took the reins of the horse as Aidan dismounted. Onyx and Ian rode up right behind him, their horses loaded down with goods they'd either traded for or purchased at the fair.

"She is his dream angel," mumbled Ian, but it was loud enough for Aidan to hear.

"Dinna start thet again, Ian or we'll get into another rumble," warned Aidan.

"What's a dream angel?" asked Niall, going to Onyx's horse and helping him untie the travel bags.

"She's a lassie Aidan saw in a dream, by usin' the Stone o' Destiny," Onyx explained.

"Should ye be sayin' thet aloud?" Renard looked cautiously toward Effie as he went to help Ian unload his horse as well.

"He already told her about the stone, so there's no need te keep it a secret." Onyx threw a travel bag over his shoulder.

"I'd love to see this Stone o' Destiny," said Effie, as Aidan helped her from the horse.

"I'll show it te ye," said Niall, coming to her and smiling. "Me name is Niall, and me friend's name is Renard."

"I'm Effie, and pleased te meet ye," she said with a smile. "Niall, I'd love to take ye up on yer offer te see the stone."

"No' now," grumbled Aidan, starting to feel irritated that she kept asking about the stone. He was also starting to get an uneasy feeling in his gut and hoped Onyx and Ian weren't right about her. If she were deceiving him, he'd never forgive himself for opening his mouth and telling her about it to begin with.

"Renard, ye and Niall take care o' the horses and supplies, and then ye are free te go join the others at the fair," Aidan told him.

"But Da willna like if we leave our post of guarding the stone." Renard shook his head.

"We'll take care o' thet now," he told him. "Ye two go and have some fun."

"Aye," said Onyx. "Mayhap if ye're lucky ye can find a dream angel at the fair as well."

"Jest dinna bring her home if she has a tail," Ian called out.

They all started laughing, and Aidan decided he needed to get away from them all right now. He stormed away, but Effie followed.

"Where are ye goin'?" she asked.

"Anywhere away from them." He headed up the hill where the clan's long-haired sheep were grazing in the fields of green grass. His squirrel followed him on the ground.

"So who exactly are those two fine laddies I jest met?" asked Effie.

"They are the chieftain's son and nephew," he said.

"Where is e'erybody else?" She looked around the deserted camp.

"There are all at the fair in Glasgow. They willna be back until the fair is o'er."

"What a shame. I would have loved te meet yer clan."

He settled himself atop a hill, and Reid climbed onto his lap. He ran his hand over the squirrel's fur as he spoke.

"Ye sound as if ye dinna plan on bein' here long, lass. I thought ye said ye had no home, so where do ye plan on goin'?"

"Oh, I didna mean it thet way. I jest meant thet . . . thet I am happy fer yer hospitality but dinna want te overstay me welcome."

"Ye are welcome te stay with the MacKeefes as long as ye like." His squirrel left his lap, and he reached out and pulled Effie towards him. She laughed and settled on the ground next to him. He then fell backwards onto the soft grass and looked up to the blue sky. She lay down next to him and did the same.

"Who are ye, Effie?"

"What do ye mean?"

He turned to look at her and drank in her beauty. He loved her smile. Her green eyes lit up like the early morning sun splashing across the rolling green mountains, and her whole face shone with life. The sunrays bounced off her bright red locks, almost seeming to make her hair glow. She intrigued him more than any lassie he'd ever met. He wanted to get to know this mysterious woman, and his heart ached for the losses she'd encountered lately.

He decided he'd be her family now that she had none. He would protect her and ask Storm when he returned if she could join the MacKeefe clan. He could give her a family again, and wanted to do that more than anything. He was sure that's what his dream meant. That she needed him. Needed his protection. And he would do just that because she was special. The Stone of Destiny showed her to him, so he knew that they were destined to be together.

"When I see ye smile like thet, Effie, it makes me want te reach out and kiss ye."

"Then why dinna ye do it?" she asked.

"Ye're sayin' ye want me to?" He never expected this after the cold reception he'd received from her last night.

"Do I have te ask?"

"But ye made it so clear last night at the loch thet ye didna want me in any shape or form."

"I was angry at the time, Aidan MacKeefe. And distracted. Ye and ye're friends had no' only given away our dinner, but were standin' there naked. It's no' e'ery day a lassie is surrounded by three naked, handsome men."

"Ye think we're handsome?" he asked. "So who do ye think is the most desirable out o' the three o' us, since ye've seen us scuddy and all?" he asked, holding his breath and waiting for her answer.

She pushed up to her elbow, reaching over and kissing him. Her long hair encompassed them, making a private tent around them as they shared their intimate moment.

Her lips were so soft and tasted like sweet nectar, and her skin was smooth and milky white. When she pulled back, she smiled again, and he saw the clouds above reflecting in her eyes. Freckles trailed across her nose and down to her cheeks, making her seem so young and innocent. He reached out and ran a finger over her freckles. Then he reached up and kissed them, trying to do it one at a time.

"Ye are so silly, Aidan MacKeefe," she said with a giggle.

"So, what is yer answer, me bonnie cailin? Who out o' me and me friends do ye find most desirable? After all, ye've seen us without clothes, so there is nothin' we can hide from ye."

"Ye've all seen me scuddy as well."

"I dinna like thet fact."

"I kent ye didna like it, by the way ye blocked me naked body from the eyes o' yer friends. I must say thet I didna even notice the others, as me eyes were fastened only on ye. If ye haveta ask who I desire, then ye really dinna ken lassies at all."

With that, she rolled over atop him and covered his body with hers. He wrapped his arms around her, and they kissed again. He found himself warming quickly, and his manhood hardened beneath her. She noticed, and daringly reached down and ran her fingers over the bulge beneath his clothes.

"Ye keep doin' thet, me angel, and I will be the one tryin' te defile ye, and no' the English."

"And I wouldna stop ye, Aidan."

"Ye wouldna?" This was too good to be true. He reached down and caressed one of her breasts as they shared another kiss. Then he rolled her off of him and straddled one leg over her. His hand was under her skirt, and he daringly slipped it upward, feeling her firm leg. She raised her leg, giving him access to explore more, and he probably would have if he hadn't heard the squeaking of his squirrel from lower down the hill. He pulled back quickly and sat up.

"What's the matter?" she asked, sitting up next to him.

"I hear Reid. He is in trouble."

"Ye mean yer squirrel? Now?" He could tell by her voice that she wanted to continue what they were doing. He did as well, but it would have to wait.

He looked across the grass and spotted Reid at the top of the hill – in the mouth of Onyx's pet wildcat.

"Nay!" he screamed, jumping to his feet. The wildcat looked up and then darted down the hill toward camp and Aidan ran after it, with Effie following.

"Ian . . . Dagger," he called to alert his friends at camp. They looked up and saw what was happening. "The damn cat is goin' te kill Reid!"

His friends rushed toward the animals too, but Tawpie, Onyx's wildcat, made a turn and headed back up the hill – and stopped when a wolfhound met her head on. The hound snarled at the wildcat and showed its teeth, and Tawpie dropped the squirrel to the ground. The wildcat's fur stood on end, and she showed her sharp teeth as well.

"Look, it's thet wolfhound that almost attacked me last night," shouted Effie.

"I'll protect ye." Aidan pulled his dagger from his belt and rushed forward, but before he could make it there, Ian ran up the hill and threw himself atop the hound, bringing it to the ground. He wrestled it with his bare hands. Onyx rushed over and picked up the squirrel, and the cat slinked away towards camp.

"Use yer dagger," called out Aidan, rushing to join his friends. "The thing is possessed."

"Nay, I dinna want te hurt it," Ian called back, rolling over and over on the ground with the wolfhound in his hands. The animal snarled and tried to bite him, but eventually gave up in a whimper. It lay there under Ian's hold, and slowly he released the animal. It just looked up to him with wide eyes and Ian carefully reached out and ran a hand over its head.

"What are ye doin'?" asked Aidan, coming to his side. "Thet thing is dangerous."

"Nay," Ian said stubbornly, sitting down next to it. The animal got up quickly, looked at them with wide eyes and hurried away with a slight limp over the hills.

"Reid!" said Aidan, collecting the squirrel from Onyx. It was bleeding and barely moving. "Yer damned cat almost killed me squirrel," he shouted.

"But it didna," said Onyx.

"Only because the wolfhound saved it," added Ian.

"Ye shoulda killed thet feral thing yesterday." Aidan felt furious at this whole situation. "Now it followed us te camp and we have more problems."

"Nay," said Ian. "It is already injured and I was tryin' te help. The hound is all alone. I feel sad fer it. I think it's only tryin' te attack because it's scared. And mayhap Onyx's cat shoulda killed yer squirrel instead."

"Me cat didna mean any harm," said Onyx in his pet's defense.

"Stop yer bickerin' ye dunderheids and give me the squirrel." Effie stood with her arms outstretched, waiting for Aidan to hand over his pet.

"He's almost deid," said Aidan sadly.

"I can see thet," she said, pulling it from his hands. "If ye three fools keep up yer bickerin' it's goin' te be deid afore we can help it."

"Do ye ken how te heal animals?" asked Aidan.

"I told ye, I am a gypsy. I ken a lot o' things ye have no idea about. Now there are some herbs and things I'm goin' te need, and I need ye three to get them fer me. Aidan, get some hot water and rags, and Onyx, ye start a fire and cook some food, as I'm famished. Ian, I'll tell ye where the herbs are and what they look like, and ye make sure te keep thet hound away from here. And if I see that wildcat anywhere near this squirrel again, I swear I'll be servin' it roasted on a spit fer our next meal. Now do ye all understand what ye're te do? If we're goin' te save this poor animal's life we need te move quickly."

She took off at a good clip down the hill toward the cottages with the nearly lifeless, bloody squirrel in her hands, not bothering to wait for an answer.

Aidan and his friends just stood there with their mouths open and stared at each other.

"What jest happened?" asked Ian.

"Get a move on it," she shouted over her shoulder, "we don't have all day."

"Did she jest really tell us what te do?" asked Aidan.

"I think she did," said Ian, shaking his head in disbelief.

"And I thought me bairned wife was moody and demandin'. Aidan, ye got yerself a live one there." Onyx scratched the back of his neck and watched Effie rushing down the hill.

"I guess so," Aidan said.

"What're ye goin' te do about it?" asked Ian.

"Reid's life is in danger," Aidan replied. "Do we really have a choice? Ye heard her, now let's get movin'."

CHAPTER 8

*E*ffie woke the next morning, taking a moment to realize where she was. She looked around and found herself lying on a pallet in a darkened cottage. A small table with a few chairs were across the room as well as several other pallets, and some personal belongings such as trunks and clothing. There was a fire pit in the center of the room but with no fire, as it was summer. Above it, there was a thatched roof that came to a v, with holes in the sides at the top to let out smoke, but yet keep the hut protected so that rain would not enter.

She felt something on her chest, and looked down to see Aidan's squirrel curled up atop her. She'd spent all night holding it outside by the fire, applying her poultices and herbs, and trying to save its life.

She couldn't have done it without the help of the three madmen, and had almost laughed at the way those three big, strong men were jumping at her command, and running around collecting the things she needed. She knew now that they all had a side to them that wasn't as harsh as they sometimes let on.

The last she remembered she was dozing off, leaning back into Aidan's protective embrace with the squirrel curled up on her lap as they sat under the stars. Aidan must have brought her here to sleep, and she'd been so tired that she hadn't even noticed.

The door to the cottage opened, and there stood Aidan with a smile on his face and holding something behind his back. In his other hand he held a bowl of food and a spoon.

"Guid mornin' me bonnie angel," he said, entering the room.

"Thank ye fer bringin' me here last night." Sitting up, she took the squirrel off her chest. She removed the wrapping of cloth that she'd put around it to hold closed its wounds.

"How is Reid?" he asked, entering the room and closing the door with his foot extended behind him. The sunshine that had been streaming into the little cottage disappeared.

"He is goin' te survive, thanks te the help ye and yer friends gave me last night."

The squirrel shook its head and stretched. Then it licked its wounds, flicked its tail, and scurried off the pallet to inspect the floor.

"I dinna ken how I can e'er repay ye fer savin' me pet's life."

"Ye dinna have to. I only did what anyone would."

He put the bowl of food and spoon on the table and headed over to the pallet. "I brought ye food te break the fast. It is cabbie claw. I made it meself from the rest o' the fish ye caught."

Effie was familiar with the dish, which was cod fillets covered by an egg sauce and topped off with horseradish. "Well, that sounds wonderful, but I could join the rest o' ye at the fire. I dinna need me food brought te me."

"Happy Birthday, me angel." He whipped out a large bouquet of wildflowers from behind his back and handed it to her. It consisted of purple heather, pink foxglove, and even a large lilac-colored thistle sticking up from the center.

"Och," she gasped in delighted surprise, taking it from him but being careful not to touch the prickly thistle. "They're beautiful." She started to get up, but he sat down on the pallet next to her instead. He took her hands in his, and raised them up so she could smell the flowers. Closing her eyes, she took a sniff and then let out her breath. "No one has e'er given me flowers fer me birthday," she said with a tear in her eye.

"I told ye I want te fill thet empty void in yer life. Since ye have no one left from yer family or yer clan o' gypsies, I am goin' te be the one te take care o' ye today."

"Oh, ye really dinna have te do thet." She felt horrible now for lying to him, and she didn't deserve any of this. She tried to get up, but he took the flowers, placing them down, and held her on the pallet. Reaching over, he kissed her. She found herself lost not only in his kiss, but in the kindness of someone caring for her and making her feel special.

"I want te take care o' ye, Effie. Ye saved me squirrel, and I am e'er so grateful."

"Well, ye saved me life, twice now, so I guess we are even."

"I have a present fer ye, too."

"A present? Och, no, I couldna accept it."

"Aye, ye can." He reached over to the foot of the pallet and opened a trunk. He pulled out a woman's long white leine with billowing sleeves and a sleeveless kirtle. The skirt was brown but the bodice was made from the same beautiful purple and green plaid that he wore.

Her hands reached out instinctively, and she took them. "What is this?" she asked.

"Yer own clothes are soiled and ripped. Ye need somethin' clean and nice te wear on yer birthday, lass."

"But . . . these are the clothes of someone from yer own clan." The thought of it warmed her heart and scared her at the same time.

"They are only clothes, lass."

"It is the same purple and green plaid that ye wear, as well as the rest o' the MacKeefes."

"Our auld weaver only kens how te make one type. Thet's why

the MacKeefes all have the same plaid."

"The dyes for the wool alone must be so expensive."

"Nay, our weaver dyes the clooth herself. She uses things such as nettle and bracken fer the green and her favorite is makin' the purple dye from bilberries, whortleberries and even sea slugs, believe it or no'."

"Sea slugs?" she asked, laughing.

"Come on, Effie, jest put them on."

"But . . . I am no' part o' yer clan, Aidan."

"Ye will be part o' the clan as soon as I talk te our chieftain when he returns, and ask him if ye can join the MacKeefes." He smiled and looked so happy that she thought she was going to die.

"Aidan . . . I dinna think I could."

"O' course ye can, me angel."

"Where did you get them?"

"They are extra clothes o' me sister, Kyla, but she willna mind, I assure ye."

She looked down to the clothes, thinking how much she wanted to belong to a family again. To his family – his clan. She missed that sense of belonging, but she couldn't take them and wear them. Not when she was about to deceive him, and be a traitor to Scotland as well.

"I'd rather no' wear them." She pushed them back into his hands.

"Then I will dress ye meself," he said, reaching out to touch her. She was going to object, until she felt his hot breath on the side of her cheek as he placed sensual kisses on the back of her neck and then around and down to her collar bone.

Squeezing her eyes closed, she held her breath. It felt good. Too damned good, and it scared her.

"What's the matter, lassie, dinna ye want me te do this?"

"I . . . I'm fine," she said with a deep sigh. She looked into his eyes, seeing that he trusted her and that he had feelings for her as well. She felt the same way about him. If only she could tell him about her sister and what she had to do to save her. But if word got out, her sister's life would be endangered.

Besides, if Aidan knew the truth, he was just mad enough to go with his friends to Liddel Castle and try to save her sister himself, and in the process he would most likely be killed. She couldn't have that. These men didn't deserve to lose their lives, especially for someone they didn't even know.

No, she decided. She'd keep her secret and just go forward with the plan. Once her sister was free, she'd be able to tell Aidan everything. Only, by then, sadly, it might be too late to save what they had between them.

"Jest say the word, and I'll stop," he told her, his mouth now on her chest with his tongue shooting out to taste her. "Ye are me angel, Effie, and nothin' can change thet. I have waited a lifetime te find someone like ye."

"How can ye say thet, when ye've jest met me?" Her breathing deepened as he took his finger and drew a circle over her nipple right through her clothes.

"I ken ye are special and thet ye were meant te be with me, because ye came te me in a dream."

"Mayhap it was someone else." She felt her nipple tighten, and a bolt of desire shot through her as he slid his hand inside the neckline of her bodice and his cool fingers caressed her breast. The hot skin of her body against his cool hand made her arch her back, pushing herself further into his embrace.

"Nay, it was ye, I am sure."

"How can you be sure?" She let out a soft whimper as Aidan gently pushed aside her bodice and lowered his head to her bosom. He took her into his mouth and his tongue teased her peak, about driving her out of her mind. Gripping his hair tightly in anticipation, she was frightened for more reasons than one. She'd never made love to a man before, and she didn't want to disappoint him.

He raised his head slightly, his eyes looking up to her. "I ken it was ye, because I saw in me dream the birthmark on yer arm." He reached over and grabbed her arm and pulled away her sleeve to prove his point.

"Well, a lot o' people have birthmarks."

"No' like this one, lassie. Yers looks like a skull."

"A skull?" When she turned her arm to look at it from his direction, she realized what he said was true. She also felt like it meant death, and she didn't want anyone dying because of her.

"I better get up now," she said, trying to sneak out from under him.

"No' until I give ye yer birthday present." He gently pushed her back down on the pallet.

"But ye already have. The clothes and the flowers."

"Nay, there is more."

"What more could there possibly be?" Her body was tingling and she was trying to ignore it.

He unfastened his weapon belt and threw it to the floor. His clothes followed. He didn't wear any braies, and her eyes dropped to his straightened manhood that was hot, hard, and ready.

"I am yer present, me angel, if ye'll have me."

Her body shook with anticipation, and she felt a wetness between her thighs that was brought on by his foreplay as well as the fact he was straddling her in the nude, offering himself as her present.

She was far too old for never having had a man, as most girls her age were married while very young and had at least several children by now. She had no husband, and no children, and she didn't want to die without feeling the ecstasy of coupling with someone at least once in her lifetime. All thoughts of her sister temporarily were swept from her mind, and she knew this may not be moral right now, but she also knew she had to have him.

"This'll be the best present I e'er got in me life," she said with a slight smile.

"Then let me help ye." He reached out and pulled her clothes from her body so quickly that she knew in the back of her mind that he was very experienced with women.

"I . . . I'm scared," she blurted out, and he just stopped and looked at her with an odd expression on his face.

"I am no' goin' te hurt ye," he assured her.

"I didna mean it thet way."

"Then what did ye mean?" He settled himself atop her, and she almost cried out in passion when she felt his warm, naked body pressed up against hers. The proof of his desire prodded her, and she suddenly realized he was so big and she so small, that she didn't know if she could actually take him into her body. She clamped her legs together quickly.

"Effie, what is the matter?" he asked. "Ye are shakin' like a virgin."

"I am."

"Ye are . . . shakin' . . . or a virgin?" he asked slowly.

"Both."

"Och!" He sat up suddenly and ran a weary hand through his long, blond hair. "I'm sorry, I didna ken." He started to scoot off of her, but she reached out and clasped her hands around his arms.

"Nay! I dinna want ye te leave."

"Effie, I dinna think I am the man ye want te take from ye somethin' thet ye'll ne'er be able te get back."

She thought about that, and knew that she would be taking something from him that he'd never get back either once the stone was gone. She also knew that if she only made love once in her entire life, she wanted it to be with Aidan.

"Ye're exactly who I want te take me virginity. Now, please, give me the present ye promised me fer me birthday."

"Are ye sure, lassie? Because it is no' too late te change yer mind."

"I am sure. I want ye, Aidan. I want ye more than I've e'er wanted anyone in me life. Now please. Just be gentle, but show me how it feels te make love. Please."

"Gladly." He smiled just then, and for one glorious moment she felt like everything was going to be all right. Even if it wasn't, she didn't want to believe it right now. Instead, she decided to embrace the moment and make this so special that she'd never forget it for as long as she lived.

"I'm no' really sure how te do this," she admitted.

"By the rood, are ye tellin' me a stoater like ye ne'er even had a man touch ye?"

"I am glad ye think I am stunnin', but I assure ye while many laddies have tried, I warded them all off."

"Why would ye?"

"Because, I was busy bein' a mathair to me wee sister."

"Well, ye no longer need te do thet, so now ye need te think o' yerself. Just lay back and close yer eyes."

"Close me eyes?" She didn't want to do that. "I dinna want te miss a second o' this, after I've waited so long fer this day."

"All right. Mayhap thet is a better idea. Instead, I want ye te take a look at e'ery wee bit o' me." He stood then, spreading his legs on each side of her, and shaking his pelvis slightly, letting her see all of him. Then he turned slowly and showed her his backside too, shaking his doup as well.

"I like what I see," she admitted. "And believe me, no bit o' ye is wee anywhere. Now tell me. Do ye like what ye see as well?"

"I dinna ken. Stand up here and join me and shake what ye have, and I will tell ye."

"All right," she said, laughing, standing atop the pallet and holding on to him so she wouldn't fall. She moved slightly, and he just smiled and shook his head.

"Blethers, thet is no' a shake, but a shimmy. Now shake it like a wench who is tryin' te lure me to her bed."

"Like a hoor, ye mean?"

"Och," he said and smiled. "I suppose I'm no' goin' about this right." He reached out and filled his hands with her breasts, and she liked the way it felt. "I was jest tryin' to make ye ready."

"Let me try te do this." She pushed his hands away slightly, then shook her shoulders, which caused her breasts to bounce back and forth. She smiled when she noticed his eyes widen in delight. "Is this excitin' ye?"

"Dinna ye see me man sword o' love?" he asked, which caused her to giggle more. "If ye keep shakin' yer diddies like thet, I'll no' be able te wait much longer."

"Then dinna wait," she said, reaching up and wrapping her arms around his shoulders. "Make love te me now, Aidan."

She didn't have to ask again. He reached down and took her face in his hands and kissed her deeply. Then he let his hands slip slowly down her back and he gently lowered her to the pallet.

"I feel somethin' happenin'," she said, throwing back her head as he straddled her, letting his hand slide up between her legs.

"Yer body is gettin' ready te take me," he explained.

"Is thet – ye?" she asked, her heart racing in her chest, as she felt herself being entered.

He laughed then, and pulled back his hand. "Nay, lassie, thet was only me finger. Then he replaced his finger with a part that she didn't even question was him. He entered her and stopped, reaching down to fondle her breast, and kissed her atop the head at the same time.

"Thet is ye now, I can tell," she said in a breathy voice.

"No' all o' me." He pushed slowly into her, stretching her small form to take all of him into her body. She knew the emptiness within her had been filled in more ways than one. Then he started moving his hips slowly in a thrusting action. His breathing deepened and she looked up to see passion on his face. He entered her and retreated, the motions starting slowly, and then becoming faster as he pushed into her over and over again.

She felt a new feeling encompassing her being as her body

cried out for him, and she felt as if she couldn't get enough of this wonderful, glorious man.

"Aidan, I like this," she admitted. Her body was vibrating and she felt so reckless. Every bit of her tingled, and she had never felt so alive in her entire life.

"I told ye, ye would," he said through heavy breathing. Before she knew what was happening, her head was spinning and she was trying to take him into her more than he would go.

"Och, Aidan, this feels so guid." She wrapped her arms around his neck and pulled herself toward him.

"Now let yerself release any fears, lassie and ye will feel the closest thing te heaven thet ye've e'er felt." He picked her up while on his knees and settled her legs around his waist as they continued.

She did as he said and together they found release, and she felt for the first time in her life that she'd found the man she wanted to spend the rest of her life with. Her heart raced and her chest heaved as she struggled to regain her breath from her wonderful experience. He pulled away then, and lay her back down on the pallet, and when he did, her head fell back on something hard.

"Ow!" she said, pushing up and looking behind her. "What was thet?"

"'Twas nothin', angel," he told her. "Jest me pillow."

"Pillow?" she said and laughed. "Thet's no pillow, as it felt like a rock." She moved the pallet aside and looked underneath, and there embedded halfway into the ground was a thick, black stone. She knew exactly why it felt like a rock now, because it *was* a rock. She'd just found the very thing that would free her sister, and it was right there in Aidan's bed as they made love. It was the exact thing she'd been searching for and also the last thing she wanted to see at this intimate moment. This was the object that could save her sister yet make her lose Aidan forever. "Thet's no pillow," she said. "Thet is the Stone o' Destiny."

CHAPTER 9

"Aye, thet is the Stone o' Scone, or the Stone o' Destiny as most people call it." Aidan lay next to Effie, feeling sated and happy. He knew now it was no mistake bringing her here, as he felt like they were meant for each other. And if he had anything to say about it, she was never going to leave.

"Ye really sleep on it," she said with a smile, rubbing her head.

"Ye get used te it after six months," he told her, and pulled away the pallet so she could view the coronation stone better.

"'Tis beautiful." She reached out cautiously and ran her fingers over it. "And there's some sort o' etchings on it."

"They say they are hieroglyphs, or some sort of auld writin' from ancient Egypt," Aidan explained.

"Egypt?" she asked. "Ye dinna really believe thet?"

"Why no'? After all, Jacob from the Bible used the stone as a pillow and had dreams o' angels, and thet's exactly what happened te me."

"Ye dreamt o' me, no' an angel," she reminded him.

"Thet's why ye are me angel, Effie." He ran his fingers softly over her cheek, and she closed her eyes and shuddered slightly. "Isna it hard te believe thet stone is so auld thet it was used in the coronation o' e'ery king o' Scotland, fer the last five hundred years?"

"So this must be the stone me grandmathair used te coronate Robert the Bruce, after King Edward stole the fake stone," said Effie in admiration.

"Yer grandmathair?" asked Aidan, pushing up to a sitting position on the pallet. "Effie, are ye sayin' ye are related by bluid te Isabel MacDuff?"

"Aye," she answered with a nod of her head. "So ye've heard o' her?"

"Me angel, e'eryone kens about Isabel. If it wasna fer her, Scotland would most likely be ruled by those English bastards right now. Ye should be honored te be her kin. I heard the poor lassie was kept in a cage fer four years out in all kinds o' weather, and in view of all fer what she'd done. I canna even imagine a lassie put in a cage. Thet is horrible. But I didna ken she had bairns after thet. I thought once the English released her, she died."

"Thet is what she wanted e'eryone te think, Aidan. She went inte hidin' and lived with the gypsies, birthin' me mathair before she truly passed away."

"Did ye e'er have a chance te meet her?" asked Aidan with wide eyes.

"Nay, but I wish I had. She was a strong woman who stood up fer what she believed. She even went against her own husband, John Comyn. When he sided with the English, she came back te Scotland te crown Robert the Bruce king, since it was her birthright, being a MacDuff and all."

"I kent there was somethin' special about ye, Effie. Now thet yer sister is deid, ye are the only one te carry on the honors o' yer grandmathair. I am proud te say I ken ye." He reached over and kissed her, but she seemed suddenly tense. "What's the matter, angel?"

"Nothin'," she said and her head dropped down, almost as if

she were ashamed of something, though at this moment she should be very proud. "I . . . guess I'm jest missin' me sister, thet's all."

"I am sorry fer yer loss," he said. "It's no' easy te lose a loved one. But at least ye didna have te watch her hang in a cage, like what the English did te yer grandmathair."

EFFIE TRIED her hardest to keep her emotions hidden, but it wasn't easy with the way Aidan was praising her as if she were a hero when she was about to be one of the biggest traitors Scotland ever had.

She wanted more than anything to carry on her grandmother's legacy, and be the savior of Scotland so to speak. But because of her actions, instead the MacDuff name would go down in history as being black hearted, traitorous and an ally of the bloody English.

"Is thet a tear I see?" Aidan reached out and brushed away the tear from her cheek with his thumb. "Lassie, what's the matter?"

"Aidan – I was jest thinkin' about what ye said, and how horrible it must o' been fer me grandmathair te be in thet cage and all." She couldn't stop thinking of Coira, and hoped she was all right. "If ye had someone ye loved hangin' in a cage – a lassie – what would ye do?"

"I'd free her and kill those English bastards in a heartbeat."

"But . . . what if there were too many o' them, and ye would possibly lose yer life in the process?"

"If it was someone I loved, and she were a helpless lassie who had risked her own life te help her country, the way Isabel did, I would gladly give me life te save her."

"Thet's what I thought ye'd say." She knew now she couldn't tell Aidan about her sister, or that she, herself, had been imprisoned in a cage. If so, he'd be a madman enough to try to go after the bastards, and would surely lose his life in the process.

"I dinna want ye so sad on yer birthday, me angel." He got up and walked to the table to get the bowl of food. "Reid, get away from the birthday meal I've prepared fer Effie. Ye dinna eat cabbie claw, now shoo." He brushed the squirrel away from the food, and the animal scolded him in return, flicking his tail. "Well, I'm glad te see ye are back te yer ornery auld self."

He brought the food to the pallet and settled down beside her. "Try this, I made it meself."

She felt so awful right now, that a knot formed in her stomach. She looked back to the Stone of Destiny, knowing this stone would be her destiny after all. "I dinna think I could eat right now," she told him.

"Then let me help ye." He took a spoonful of food and popped it into her mouth. Wonderful flavor exploded on her tongue, and she realized this man was talented with cooking. "It's . . . really guid," she said, swallowing and licking her lips. "I had no idea ye had such talents."

"I'll show ye more talents as soon as we're finished. I am goin' te practice me caber toss this mornin' so I can beat Storm at the Highland Games competition. He has held the title fer the last ten years."

"I'd like te see thet," she said, feeling better, and digging into the food."

"Then ye will join us at the festival."

She stopped chewing and looked up slowly. She wanted to be there more than anything, but she knew her stay here was going to be short. Any day now, Tasgall would show up with the English and her time with Aidan would be over.

"I . . . dinna ken if I'll be here then," she said.

"O' course ye will, Effie. As soon as I ask Storm if ye can be a part o' our clan, ye'll be one o' the MacKeefes. Ye'll have a new family te replace the one ye lost."

She just looked down and shook her head. She knew this would never be.

"Och, I'm sorry, lassie. I didna mean te make ye sad about yer family." He took her hand in his and with the fingers of his other hand, he raised her chin and looked into her eyes. "I ken this is crazy, Effie, but I have always been a madman, so I'm jest goin' te say it. I think I love ye, angel, and I dinna want ye te leave me side. So please, stay."

"Love?" She jerked back so quickly that the food fell off her lap to the pallet.

"Did I say somethin' wrong?" he asked, scooping the food back into the bowl.

"Nay . . . I jest didna expect thet."

"I ken it is crazy, lass, but I feel as if ye've been brought te me fer a reason."

"Oh, I can say thet is probably true." Little did he know the real reason.

"The stone brought us together," he said with a smile, rubbing his hand over the smooth rock.

"Again, I'd have te agree with ye there."

There was a knock at the door, and Effie looked up quickly. "Dinna let yer friends in afore I'm dressed," she said, reaching for her torn and worn clothes. "I dinna care te let them see me naked a second time."

"Aidan, are ye in there?" came a girl's voice from the other side of the door.

"Kyla, ye ken I told ye ne'er te come in unless ye knock and are invited."

"Thet's why I'm knockin', now can I enter?"

"Dinna come in unless ye want te see yer brathair naked."

"Is thet yer sister?" Effie asked.

"Aye," he said, pulling on his clothes hurriedly. "She must o' come back from the fair early."

"Is Ian in there with ye, brathair?" His sister's muffled voice was heard from the other side of the door.

"Nay, he and Dagger are huntin' fer food."

"Why do ye call yer friend, Dagger?" asked Effie curiously. "And why does he have such odd eyes?"

"I dinna ken why his eyes are two different colors. He was born thet way," said Aidan, pulling his clothes into place. "Dagger is what Onyx's close friends call him, e'er since he was found in a box with a dagger when he was a bairn."

"He was?" asked Effie.

"I'll have him tell ye the story sometime." He didn't bother to wear shoes, and stood up quickly. "Get dressed and meet me in the field outside the cottage, and I'll show ye how I toss a caber."

"All right," she said, starting to don her old clothes. He reached out and grabbed the new MacKeefe clothes and held them out to her. "No' those auld clothes, wear these instead."

She looked up to him and saw the hope in his eyes. Wearing them would be like accepting the fact he'd just said he loved her and wanted her to stay with him. It would be like saying she wanted to be one of them – which she did.

"I dinna ken, Aidan." When she looked up to him again, she saw sadness in his eyes, and his face took on a dour disposition. Something tugged at Effie's heart and she felt as if she were going to cry. She didn't want to disappoint him, but neither did she want to lead him on with hopes of something that could never be. She couldn't wear his sister's clothes when she was about to betray them. The MacKeefes were the family she always wanted, but she didn't deserve these wonderful people in her life.

Her eyes went to her old clothes and settled on the MacDuff brooch, and she felt a whole new aching within her heart. How could she wear them after Aidan had told her how proud she should be after what her grandmother had done? She didn't deserve to dress like a MacDuff either. Not with what she was about to do. The MacDuffs stood for the heritage of Scotland - pride, determination, and doing anything to show their loyalty to their king and the land they loved, not betraying their king and country.

Either way, she was doomed. She only wished she had a third option right now. Perhaps she should just walk around naked. She sat there just staring at the clothes, not knowing what to do.

"Aidan, what are ye doin' in there?" came Kyla's voice from outside the door. "I'm comin' in."

Effie quickly grabbed the MacKeefe clothes from Aidan and held them in front of her body when his sister opened the door and burst inside. The girl stopped, and jerked backward when she saw Effie.

"Ye werena jestin' about all thet naked stuff, were ye?" she asked her brother.

"I told ye no' te come in," he said, scowling at his sister. "Why dinna ye go find and pester Ian and Dagger like ye usually do?"

"I'm Kyla," the girl said, ignoring her brother and smiling kindly at Effie.

"I'm . . . Effie." She felt very awkward.

"Are those me clothes?" she asked, looking first at the clothes in Effie's hands and then back to her brother.

"She disna have anythin' te wear, Kyla. I didna think ye'd mind."

"Well, then I suppose ye willna mind thet I gave yer horse te Wren's brathair, Madoc, either, will ye?"

"Me horse? Madoc? What are ye talkin' about ye mischant lass?"

"I got a ride here with Madoc and came back from the fair early. He jest came te check on his birds and he is leavin' again right away."

"Ye canna give away me horse, Kyla. Why disna he use his own?"

"His horse went lame jest as we arrived, and he said he disna have time te wait and see if it'll heal. His wife, Abbey is birthin' their third bairn any day now, and he wants te get back te Blake Castle te be with her."

"Bid the devil, ye are always causin' trouble, Kyla. Where is Madoc? I'll go talk with him."

"He's gone te the pigeon roost te take care o' his birds."

Aidan collected his squirrel from the table and rushed out the door, leaving Effie and Kyla there, just looking at each other awkwardly.

"So ye're Aidan's sister," Effie said, surveying the girl. She looked to be around the same age as herself, and had light brown hair that was tied back and trailed down to her waist. Her big, brown eyes were round with wonder as she surveyed Effie as well.

"I am," she said, closing the door behind her. "And who exactly are ye? Another one o' me brathair's hoors?"

"I'm no' a hoor," Effie snapped, though she felt no better than one lounging naked on the pallet with a bowl of food at her feet.

"Then why did Aidan bring food te his bed, no' te mention give ye me clothes?"

"It's me birthday," she said. "He was jest tryin' te be nice te me. He saved me from English curs who were goin' te accost me. I'm a gypsy who jest had me whole clan killed by the English. I may be a lot o' things, but I assure ye, I am no' a hoor. This was me first time te e'er lay with a man fer yer information." She jumped up from the pallet and threw the clothes at Kyla, and turned back and started to don her old, ripped and dirtied ones.

"Och, I'm sorry. Me brathair and his friends usually have a lot o' lassies, and I dinna like it. I didna mean te judge ye."

"It disna matter." She pulled on the dirtied clothes and fastened her brooch into place.

"What is thet brooch?" asked Kyla.

"What does it matter?"

"Let me see thet," she said, walking forward, but Effie held out her hand and stopped her.

"Ye may as well ken. I am Effie MacDuff, and this brooch was me grandmathair's," she said, running her hand over it lovingly.

"Ye're a MacDuff?" Kyla asked. "The MacDuffs are revered by the rest o' the clans because o' a lassie named –"

"Isabel MacDuff," said Effie. "I ken. The lassie was me grandmathair, but I assure ye I am no' te be admired like her."

Kyla walked over and held out the MacKeefe clothes. "Wear these," she said. "Ye shouldna wear those torn and dirtied clothes. I would be honored fer the granddaughter o' Isabel MacDuff te wear me clothes."

Effie stopped and looked at the girl. She was smiling now, and her features reminded Effie a little of her own sister. She missed Coira so much and worried about her every minute. She had always confided in her sister when she was feeling sad, and it felt good to have another woman around right now.

"Are ye sure?" she asked. "They are yer clothes, and I really dinna deserve them."

"I'm sure o' it. I like ye. Ye are different than the rest o' the lassies me brathair usually beds. I can see why he likes ye. Put them on and let's go find Ian."

"All right," she said, taking the clothes gingerly and doing as the girl suggested. "But dinna ye mean let's go find Ian and Onyx too?"

"Och, aye. Thet's what I meant." The girl's face blushed and she looked the other way.

"I heard ye ask fer Ian at the door as well."

"It was nothin', she said. "I jest wondered where they were."

"Does Aidan ken how ye feel about his friend, Ian?" She busied herself dressing in the MacKeefe clothes, liking the way they felt. Then she took her grandmother's brooch, and carefully placed it on the table. There was no way she could wear it right now.

"I didna say thet." Once again, Kyla's face blushed.

"Ye didna have te say it. I have a younger sister, and ye remind me o' her. I've seen her act this same way o'er a laddie she once liked."

"Ye have a sister? What's her name?"

"Coira."

"Where is she? Is she here too?"

"Nay, she's been taken captive by the English."

Suddenly, Effie realized her mistake. She'd been so distracted with the clothes and the fact she actually had another female to talk to, that she'd accidentally told Kyla about Coira. And it was too late now to take it back.

"She has?" gasped Kyla. "Thet's terrible. Mayhap Aidan can help ye get her back."

"Nay. Kyla, dinna say anythin' about this te anyone. Please."

"Why no'? she asked. "I'd think ye'd want some help in tryin' te free her."

"I dinna need anyone riskin' their life fer me or me sister. Now, please promise me ye willna say a word about it. Especially te Aidan."

"But I'm sure Aidan would want te help ye."

"How would ye feel when Ian went with him, and if neither o' them came home alive?"

"Och, I see yer point." The girl's head lowered and she looked to the floor.

"Ye keep me secret about me sister, and I'll keep yer secret thet ye have eyes fer Ian. Is it a deal?"

Kyla looked up and smiled. "It's a deal. I dinna want ye te lose yer sister, but neither do I want te lose Ian or me brathair or any o' his friends."

"Neither do I," she said, looking over to the Stone of Destiny. "Neither do I."

CHAPTER 10

*a*idan was delighted when he saw his sister and Effie opening the door to the pigeon loft, and coming inside to join them. Effie had donned the clothes he gave her after all, and she looked good wearing them. Almost as if she were a MacKeefe. But for some reason, she hadn't used her MacDuff brooch.

"Me angel," he said, holding out his hand. She took his hand in hers and joined him and Madoc at the roost. Madoc raised homing pigeons, and also raced them.

"Your angel?" asked Madoc, laughing. "Now that's the first I've ever heard that."

"She is me dream angel," said Aidan. "I saw her in a dream, while I was sleepin' on the Stone o' Destiny."

"You sound so smitten with the girl. But if you really saw her in a dream, then I guess she is your destiny," said Madoc. "Just like my wife, Abbey, was my destiny the day I robbed her on the road."

"You robbed someone?" asked Effie.

"I used to be a thief," he said, walking forward to greet her. He let go of one of the pigeons in his hand and it fluttered up high to the rafters. "My name is Madoc," he said. "And who are you?"

"Effie." Effie held out her hand and the handsome man took it and kissed it. He was tall with long, dark hair that fell around his shoulders. His eyes were bright green and mysterious, and he had a sword at his side, and the crest of an eagle on his tunic.

"Effie, this is Wren's brathair," said Aidan. "He used te be a thief afore he found out he was really o' noble English blood."

"I see." She pulled her hand back quickly, hearing the part of him being English.

"You don't seem to like the fact I'm English," said Madoc.

"I'm sorry," she said. "I didna mean te be rude, but the English jest killed off me family."

"Your family?" he asked, surveying her clothes. "So you are not a MacKeefe?"

"Nay, I'm Effie MacDuff, and if ye please, I'd no' like te talk about it any more."

"Of course," he said, looking at her oddly. "I'm sorry."

"What are all these birds fer?" she asked, looking around. Effie was standing inside a small, wooden hut with a tall ceiling. Pigeons sat roosting on the rafters above their heads. There were other birds that looked to be nesting, and still more that were in separate enclosures.

"These are homing pigeons," Madoc told her. "I raise them." The pigeons in the separate cages are messengers. They are the ones that fly to my brother's castle in Devonshire, to the MacKeefe's castle, or to my twin sister's home in Hythe."

"Madoc has pigeons in e'ery place one o' his siblings lives," Aidan explained. "Thet is how they send messages between them, and from England te Scotland and back."

"Fascinatin'," she said. "So do ye have pigeons near the border-lands too?" She wondered if any of them were near to Liddel

Castle where her sister was being held captive. If so, this may come in handy somehow.

"I do," Madoc said with a smile. "The MacKeefe's castle, Hermitage Castle, in on the border. And since my sister, Wren, sometimes dwells there, I have birds there as well. Actually, I am going there next, as I need to return pigeons that are trained to fly one way only. That will be my last stop. Why do you ask?"

"No reason. Jest curious," she said.

"It is several days ride to the border," he said, looking at Aidan. "I'd like to leave as soon as possible. Since my horse went lame, I was hoping to borrow one of your clan's horses, but I understand they are all gone, as your clan is still at the Glasgow fair."

"Thet's right," said Aidan. "Why dinna ye jest stay till they return?"

"My wife, Abbey, is going to give birth soon to our third child," he said. "I'm anxious to get back to her. We have both a boy and a girl already, and I'm hoping this one is another son. I really want to raise as many sons as I can, since I grew up without a father. Kyla offered me your horse, Aidan, but I really hate to take it on you."

"Nay, take me horse," said Aidan with sigh. "It is important te be there fer yer wife and new bairn. I'll come te collect me horse and return yers when it's healed. I'll return it te ye personally at Blake Castle, and hopefully see yer new bairn as well."

"My many thanks," said Madoc. "I'll be sure to have it back to you sooner than that, as I know you're going to want it when you go to the Highland Games. And Effie, I hope to see you there as well?"

"I dinna ken." She looked at Aidan, and he had that sad look upon his face again. "Well, mayhap I'll jest do thet." Aidan smiled at those words, and it did her heart good to see his face light up again.

"Madoc, join us fer a bite te eat," said Aidan. "Afterwards, mayhap ye'd like te get inte the little competition we're havin', as we practice fer the Highland Games."

"I'd be happy to eat with you and also to watch you practice, but I'm afraid I'm not skilled in much besides wielding a sword or racing pigeons," Madoc answered. Actually, I have my brother, Corbett, to thank for me being a knight. He trained me well, since I was just a thief."

"I'd love to hear about it," said Effie.

"I'd be happy to tell you everything over a bite of food." He looked at Aidan and grinned. "Unless it's pigeon stew."

"Dinna worry," Aidan said with a chuckle. "The MacKeefes no longer eat pigeon thanks te yer sister."

"Nor do we eat squirrel, thanks te ye," said Kyla. "And squirrel stew was me favorite."

Reid chattered away from outside the pigeon loft just then, causing them all to laugh.

* * *

EFFIE ENJOYED the meal along with Aidan, Onyx, Ian, Madoc, and Kyla. They were all getting along wonderfully, laughing and enjoying some mountain magic. She was getting used to the strong whisky, and only took it in small amounts, but was surprised how Kyla kept up with drinking with the men.

"Kyla, how can ye drink so much o' this brew and still be able to stand?" Effie asked, staring down at her cup.

"I grew up doin' whate'er me brathair and his friends were doin' so it disna bother me," said the girl.

"Aye, she's one o' the boys, thet's why," said Ian. "And no lass, ye dinna do e'erythin' we do, if ye ken what I mean."

"Ye'd better no' be doin' e'erything," said Aidan to his sister, "or I'll be the first te make sure whate'er laddie is in yer bed disna make it out o' here alive."

The men laughed, but Kyla just crinkled her nose and shook

her head. "Aidan, if ye keep me away from laddies much longer, I'm goin' te die a spinster."

Effie was starting to feel at home, and it was the best feeling in the world.

"Let's jest hope no laddie e'er gives her a birthday present like I gave ye," Aidan said to Effie softly, but Madoc overheard him.

"Why didn't anyone tell me it was your birthday, my lady?" Madoc got up and walked over to her, bowing, and when he stood back up, he pulled a dove from behind her ear and handed it to her. She went to grab it, and it flew up into the sky.

"How did ye do thet?" she asked in surprise.

"Madoc is known as the Lord of Illusion," said Kyla.

"Thet's right," said Aidan. "He kens all sorts o' tricks, and can also make things disappear."

"Really?" Effie wondered what she would be called once she made the Stone of Destiny disappear. She was sure it wouldn't be anything so admirable.

"Ian, play yer bagpipes," begged Kyla.

"Nay," Ian said with a scowl on his face, putting down the bones of the pheasant they were eating, having caught it earlier that day. "I dinna feel like it."

"Come on," she said, getting up and pulling the bagpipes from behind a rock. "I happen te have them right here."

"Kyla, what are ye doin'?" Ian rolled his eyes and shook his head. "Quit yer pesterin' me already, will ye lassie?" He stretched out on the grass.

Effie could see the girl was vying for Ian's attention, though he wasn't giving it to her.

"I'll play them," Effie offered, taking them into her hands, knowing the way to get a man to react.

"Ye ken how te play bagpipes?" asked Aidan.

"I do, but I'm no' verra guid at it."

"Thet's because ye need te have a lot o' wind about ye, like Aidan," said Onyx from the other side of the fire.

"I thought you knew how to play them too," Madoc said to Onyx.

"We all do," he said.

"Then he's not the only one with wind."

They all laughed at that, and when Effie brought her mouth to the bagpipes and blew a sour note, that had them all laughing again, including her.

"Give me thet," said Onyx, taking the bagpipes and placing them under his arm, blowing into it. His wildcat came out of the shadows and settled down behind him. Effie saw Madoc petting Aidan's squirrel, and knew it would be safe from the cat.

The music was cheery and Effie found herself clapping her hands and keeping beat.

"Me lady," said Aidan, bowing and holding out his hand. "May I have this birthday dance?"

"Oh, I dinna dance," she said, shaking her head.

"It's yer birthday, now get up and dance," said Kyla, pulling her to her feet.

"Only if ye dance as well," she told the girl. "With Ian."

Kyla smiled and nodded her head. Effie winked.

"I'm no' dancin'," grumbled Ian from his position on the ground, his arm over his closed eyes.

"If the birthday girl wants ye te dance, then do it," Aidan told him.

"Come on," said Kyla, pulling Ian to his feet.

"Aidan, ye owe me fer dancin' with yer wee sister." Ian got to his feet, and shot a daggered glance to Aidan.

Effie danced with Aidan, and Kyla with Ian, and Madoc even kept the beat with his spoon against a log, as he used it as a drum.

"No' so fast," said Effie when Aidan took a hold of her and twirled her around.

"I bet ye canna do this, Ian," said Aidan, as he did an even faster step, pulling Effie around in a circle.

"Dinna challenge me te somethin' because ye ken I will win," said Ian, taking a hold of Kyla and doing the same thing. Onyx played the bagpipes faster, and Madoc picked up the rhythm on his home-made drum.

Before Effie knew it, she was dizzy from turning circles so fast, and she fell to the ground atop Aidan. Ian fell as well, with Kyla in his arms.

Effie felt happy for Kyla, as well as for herself. She felt as if she never wanted to leave MacKeefe camps for the rest of her life.

"Come on," said Onyx, putting down the bagpipes. "The caber is ready fer ye, Aidan, and I have a bet with Madoc thet ye'll win."

"What about me?" said Ian, getting to his feet, and pulling Kyla with him.

"I'll bet on ye winnin'," said Kyla proudly.

"Thanks fer the vote o' confidence, lass," he told her and patted her on the head as if she were nothing more than a child.

The men walked away toward the caber. Aidan's squirrel was on his shoulder, and Onyx's wildcat was sneaking behind in the shadows.

"He thinks o' me as a bairn," Kyla told Effie, putting her hands on her hips.

"Who?" she asked. "Ian or Aidan?"

"All o' them." Kyla threw her hands into the air in frustration. "I'll ne'er be anythin' but a bairn te them."

"Men are no' always thet aware o' when a lassie likes them," Effie told her. "Jest give it time, and I'm sure some day Ian will notice ye turned inte a woman."

"Well, Aidan noticed ye, thet's fer sure," said Kyla. "And ye two jest met. I've kent Ian me whole life, and he still disna ken I even exist."

"Sometimes, when someone is so close to another, they canna see the nose on their face," she said, putting her arm around the girl. "Now let's go watch the men make fools o' themselves tryin' te prove thet one o' them is better than another."

$\mathcal{A}$idan stood with his arms wrapped around the trunk of a tree that they'd made into a mock caber. It was heavy and long, and took three people just to get it into position.

"Come on, Aidan, ye can throw a better caber than the one Ian just tossed like a lassie," called out Onyx. It was a beautiful day, and the sky was clear blue with white puffy clouds high above the peaks of the mountains. Rolling green hills surrounded them, dotted with long-haired sheep feeding on grass in the distance. A field of purple heather trailed down to the loch. It all seemed so alive as the machairs, tall grass, speckled with bright-colored wildflowers, swayed back and forth in the gentle breeze.

"Ye say thet again," Ian warned him, "and I'll show ye how I can toss the sheaf, but it'll be ye I'm tossin' instead."

"That, I'd like to see," said Madoc, lounging in the background, with his head on a rock and his feet sprawled out in front of him. Aidan's squirrel was on his chest. Effie and Kyla sat beside him.

"All right, I'm ready." Aidan took a deep breath, and with Onyx and Ian's help, hoisted the heavy pole into position, making sure Effie was watching. And he'd just taken a step forward when

Reid scampered over and climbed upon his shoulder and then started making its way directly up the pole.

"Nay, get off o' there, ye doitit squirrel," said Aidan, moving back and forth with the pole teetering almost out of control. There was no way he could actually throw it with his squirrel now perched at the very top.

"Toss it," shouted Ian.

"Nay," cried Effie, "ye'll kill the squirrel."

"Reid, get down from there," yelled Aidan, his muscles burning from holding up so much weight.

The squirrel moved down slowly, and finally scampered back to the ground. And with another step, and his muscles twitching, Aidan tossed the caber, end over end. It was an amazingly straight throw, and it settled much further than Ian's caber toss.

"Ye did it," cried Effie, running to him and throwing herself into his arms. "Ye were wonderful, Aidan." She reached up and kissed him and he picked her up and spun her in a circle before putting her back on her feet.

"I was right," said Onyx. "Aidan is the strongest when it comes to lifting weight. Too bad I didna place coin on the bet."

"Thank you for everything," said Madoc, coming and clasping arms with Aidan. "I need to be on my way before the day gets any later. Thanks again for the use of your horse."

"Would ye mind if I travelled with ye?" asked Onyx. "I am goin' te stop in Northumberland to see me sister, Amethyst, and her husband, Marcus, fer a bit afore I head on home te check on me bairned wife."

"I'd be honored," said Madoc.

"Ian, did ye want te come fer a visit as well?" asked Onyx. "I hear Marcus's cousin, Matilda is visitin', and she is a sight fer sore eyes, I assure ye."

"Aye, I do," he said anxiously, raising his eyebrows. "But I need te pick up some things at Hermitage Castle on the way if ye dinna mind. I'll get me things." Ian headed for the cottage.

Hermitage Castle was the MacKeefes' border castle that their chieftain, Storm, captured years ago. It was a place where they stayed when they weren't in the Highlands.

"I'll go too," said Kyla, following him.

"Nay, ye'll stay here with Effie and yer brathair and stop pesterin' me," growled Ian.

"Aidan, will ye and the lassies be alright here alone guardin' the stone, or should one o' us stay?" asked Onyx.

"I'll be fine," said Aidan with a wave of his hand. "The rest o' the clan should be back any day, and the stone hasna been in danger in the last six months, so I'm sure it'll stay secure fer another day or two. Besides, no one even kens it's here."

"So the three o' us will be the only ones here te guard the stone?" asked Effie.

"Aye," said Aidan. "Why do ye ask?"

"No reason," she said, her face suddenly changing from laughter to one that seemed to Aidan a look of fear.

"I will protect ye me angel, as well as the stone, dinna worry." He put his arm around her. "After all," he whispered so only she could hear, "I would give me life if I had te no' only te keep the stone from gettin' inte the hands o' the English, but also te protect ye and me sister. The lassies thet I love."

CHAPTER 12

*I*t was early the next morning, and Effie awoke in Aidan's arms after having spent the most wonderful day of her life with him yesterday. It was by far the most anyone had ever done to celebrate her birthday. Sure, her sister Coira had brought her bouquets of wildflowers and cooked her meals as well, but Aidan gave her a present that by far surpassed that. He gave her not only his body but also his heart. That meant the world to her.

The sun was just rising and she slipped away from him silently and dressed, wanting to go prepare a meal for him and bring it back and serve him in bed the way he'd done for her yesterday. Then she planned on telling him about her sister. She couldn't keep this secret to herself any longer. He couldn't do anything crazy today, because there was only one horse in the camp at the moment, and it was lame. Besides, he would never leave the Stone of Destiny unguarded.

That would give her a few days until the rest of the clan returned to try to explain to him what she'd planned on doing, and to tell him that she no longer wanted to lie and deceive people. Especially him. By the time the chieftain and the rest of the clan returned from the fair, she hoped she'd be able to talk to him sensibly and try to think of a plan to save her sister that wouldn't get any of them killed. With a whole clan to back him up, mayhap Aidan could do something to save Coira after all.

She finished dressing and looked down at herself donned in her new clothes. Liking the way they felt, she wanted more than anything to be a part of this clan. She hoped they could get Coira and bring her back to be part of the clan as well.

She spied her brooch on the table and picked it up, wanting more than anything to wear it. Mayhap after she'd had her conversation with Aidan today, if things went well, she'd feel differently. But for now, she couldn't bring herself to pin it on her clothes. She didn't even want to look at it right now, so she reached down and slipped it under the pallet, and out of sight.

She glanced over to Aidan sleeping soundly on the pallet, his long, blond hair sprawled across the Stone of Destiny as he used it as his pillow. The stark contrast of his light hair and the black stone made her think how different the two of them were as well. Like day and night, in a way.

Aidan had said he'd give his life to protect the stone, but she was willing to give up the destiny of Scotland in order to save the life of her sister. He was so honest with her, but she'd been nothing but untruthful to him. He'd told her he loved her, but yet, she didn't return the sentiment. And while he was planning their future together, she was only trying to get through another day, not knowing if she or her sister would live to see the morrow.

She kissed him softly on the forehead, then headed out the door, closing it quietly behind her.

"Guid mornin'," said Kyla from behind her, scaring Effie and making her jump. She held her hands over her heart.

"Ye frightened me, Kyla. I didna ken ye were there."

"I'm sorry, Effie. I jest wanted te say thank ye fer gettin' Ian te dance with me yesterday, before I head down te the loch te bathe. I really wish I could o' gone with them when they left."

"It's the least I could do," she said. "After all, ye welcomed me here with open arms and even gave me yer clothes. Jest give Ian some room te breathe, as men dinna like lassies hangin' on them."

"I guess ye're right. So where are ye goin'?" Kyla asked.

"I am sneakin' out te make a guid meal fer yer brathair and surprise him by bringin' it te him in bed."

"Did he tell ye he loves ye, yet?"

"What makes ye ask thet?" Effie's voice raised in surprise. Then she walked across the camp toward the center fire pit that was used for cooking, and Kyla followed.

"Because I could see it in his eyes. It's the same look he gets when he finds a new lassie thet he thinks is special, but it ne'er lasts."

"So ye're sayin' thet Aidan has told lassies before thet he loves them?"

"He's always sayin' thet. Usually when he brings them te his bed, and then by the next mornin', the lassie leaves and he forgets all about her."

"Then it's a guid thing he didna try thet on me," she said, feeling her heart drop inside her chest. She'd thought Aidan had really cared for her, but now after hearing this, she knew it was nothing more to him than a reaction when he'd gotten a good bedding.

"Effie, I can see it in yer eyes," said Kyla with a smile. "He said he loved ye, didna he?"

"Aye," she admitted shyly, then felt filled with anger. "Thet bastard," she spat. "He even told me he wanted me te stay here with the MacKeefes. I guess he'd say anythin' te get me in his bed."

"He asked ye te stay? I've ne'er heard him say thet te any lassie afore." Kyla bent down and started collecting kindling for the fire. "It would be nice if ye stayed. Ye are like the sister I ne'er had. I like ye." She stood up and put her arm around Effie's shoulder, but Effie knew she couldn't go on with this pretense any longer. Neither did she want to stay and hear Aidan's lies if he really didn't mean what he'd said.

She removed the girl's arm from around her shoulder. "Kyla, I dinna think I'm goin' te be stayin'. Matter o' fact, I plan on leavin' really soon."

"What do ye mean? Does Aidan ken about this?"

Effie couldn't have the girl telling Aidan she planned on leaving. She didn't want to alert him to her plan. She had to say something to keep her quiet. "I mean, I really miss me sister and worry about her," she said, which wasn't a lie. "Aidan disna need te ken thet I'm no' goin' te stay. Especially since he willna care anyway, if he tells all the lassies he loves them."

"I can understand thet."

"So dinna say anythin' te him jest yet. I mean . . . I'll tell him later, all right?"

"If ye say so," she said. "Still, I will miss ye."

Effie almost cried out when she looked over Kyla's shoulder and spied Tasgall peering out at her from behind a clump of trees. He was motioning with his hand for her to join him.

"So what shall we make te break the fast?" asked Kyla, her back toward the man, so she didn't see him.

"Dinna fash yerself, I'll make the food," she said, getting to her feet. "Why dinna ye go and bathe in the loch now afore yer brathair awakes?"

"He's usually awake by now," she said, standing and straightening her skirts. "I'll go wake him if thet lazy galoot is still sleepin'."

"Nay, go get yer things and head out to the loch now." Effie turned the girl and headed her in the opposite direction from where she'd seen Tasgall. "I'll awaken Aidan."

"Are ye sure?"

"Aye," she said, picking up the bow and arrows that she'd left there yesterday. "I'm jest goin' te go hunt fer a rabbit real quick, and then I'll awake him as soon as I'm back. Jest let him sleep fer now."

"Well, all right, but jest dinna shoot Aidan's squirrel or he will have yer heid."

"I'll be careful," she said, glad that Onyx had taken his pet wildcat with him on his journey, as that animal made her a little uncomfortable. She picked up the bow and arrows and hurried toward the woods.

"What took ye so long?" growled Tasgall once she'd joined him in the woods.

"What are ye doin' here?" she snapped.

"Dinna be a fool. I brought the English soldiers like ye said." With a wave of his hand, a half-dozen English soldiers appeared, bringing a horse and cart.

Her heart beat rapidly, and she was no longer sure she really wanted to do this. Even if Aidan had lured her to his bed with the words he probably used on whores, she still didn't want to see him ending up dead. If they went for the stone right now, she knew he'd fight to the death to try to protect it.

"How did ye get te the castle and back so fast?" she asked the man.

"I didna have to. The soldiers came lookin' fer us, sent by Lord Ralston. It seems he is in a hurry to get the stone, and will be sending a missive for King Edward to join him right there at Liddel Castle soon. Lord Ralston wants te present the stone to King Edward personally, as a surprise."

"Surprise indeed," she sniffed. "He wants to be the one to take all the credit for its return and probably thinks it'll earn him a seat at court or a new title when this is all o'er."

"Whate'er his reason, I dinna care."

"What's yer reason, Tasgall fer helping do this?" She eyed him curiously. "What did Lord Ralston promise ye when this is all o'er?"

"What makes ye think he offered me anythin'?" he asked, raising his chin when he spoke.

"I find it odd thet besides me and me sister who were the only true MacDuffs, they spared yer life when they attacked and killed the rest o' the gypsies."

"Thet's because I had information about the stone," he told her. "Now, enough o' this clishmaclaver, we have a job te do. Is it safe te get the stone, or no'? We saw the rest o' the MacKeefes still at the fair, and we hid when three men left this camp yesterday, so there canna be many left. How many are there?"

"Plenty," she lied, wanting them gone. "At least a dozen or so men, so ye'd better turn around and leave if ye dinna want te be slaughtered. Highlanders are barbaric and will take all yer lives."

"That many?" Tasgall peered over her shoulder toward the camp. "Then how come I dinna see a single soul?"

She was relieved Tasgall hadn't mentioned seeing Kyla in front of all the soldiers.

"They're – all inside. Sleeping."

"Ye're lyin'," Tasgall growled. Then he looked over his shoulder to the rest of the guards. "She's obviously changed her mind about helping us, so we'll jest have to do it ourselves."

"Aye," said the soldier named Dempster from atop his horse. "We'll get the stone and kill anyone who gets in our way." He motioned with his hand for the others to follow and the entourage started to move toward the camp.

"Nay!" She said, wanting to stop them, because if she didn't, she knew both Aidan and his sister would be slaughtered. "Stop!" she called out, but they didn't listen. Then she raised her bow, nocked an arrow, and let it fly. She'd only meant to get their attention, but the arrow embedded itself in Dempster's shoulder. He winced in pain and turned around in fury.

"You bitch!" he called out, breaking off the arrow and throwing the stub to the ground. "Kill her," he said, but Tasgall pulled the bow from her hand and pushed her to the ground.

"Wait!" he said. "We may need her if we get in a bind on the way back with the stone. We'll need another Scot along besides meself if we're goin' te pull this off. Unless ye want te chance it. But a bunch o' English with a wagon travelling in the Highlands without a Scot te back up their story is goin' te raise some suspicion."

"I'm going back," said Dempster, "as I'll be no use to you now, and my wound will only cause more suspicion if we come across any Scots." He ripped off part of his tunic and held it up to his wound to stop the flow of blood. "Get the stone and bring it directly to Lord Ralston. Don't waste any time. Once you make it through the Highlands, kill her as we'll have no use for her."

"What about me sister?" she cried out. "Is Coira still alive?"

"She is," sneered Dempster. "But as soon as I tell Lord Ralston you shot me with an arrow, he'll kill her for sure. If not, I'll do the job myself to make you pay for this."

"Nay, dinna touch Coira."

"Tie her up," said Dempster, throwing a skein of rope to Tasgall.

Effie knew if she was going to save Aidan and Kyla's lives she needed to do something fast, and it wasn't looking good.

"I'll help ye get the stone," she said quickly. "Let me tie up the Highlander so he disna give ye trouble."

"How many are there?" growled another guard.

"Jest the one," she said, not wanting to tell them about Kyla, and hoping the girl didn't come back from bathing any time soon. If the guards found her, especially naked, they'd defile her, and Effie couldn't have that. She looked over to Tasgall, hoping he wasn't going to say anything, and thankfully, he didn't. "The Highlander trusts me, so I'll sneak in and tie him up and then give ye the signal," she added.

"I don't believe her," said one of the guards. "She just told us there was a dozen, now she changes her story. This is a trap."

"It's no'," she said. "Ye need te believe me."

"Why should we?" asked the guard. "You haven't proved yourself to us."

"Then let me do this te prove te ye thet me sister's life means more te me then this stone. Besides, ye dinna ken where the stone is, and I willna tell ye unless ye let me help."

She knew if she was able to tie up Aidan, it might just save his life. If not, he'd fight to the death, and she'd never forgive herself for losing the only man who ever cared for her in her life.

"All right, just let her do it, but keep an eye on her," Dempster agreed, gritting his teeth in pain. "I'm heading back to the castle, because if I don't do something about this wound soon, I'll be dead."

"We'll collect the stone and bring it back," said a guard. "Go on, we'll catch up to you."

"All right, then," said Tasgall, pushing the rope into Effie's hands. "Go tie up the Highlander, though it's beyond me how ye think ye're goin' te do it."

CHAPTER 13

*A*idan was having that dream again. He was reclining on the pallet, and saw Effie coming into the room. The sun shone around her like a halo, and though her smile was bright, he noticed this time that something troubled her.

He tried to talk, to ask her what was the matter, but couldn't seem to find the words. Reaching out to take her in his arms, he found once again he couldn't move. Then she turned back toward the door and her tail swished him in the face. When he looked up, the English were storming into his cottage.

His eyes popped open, and he jerked backward when he saw Effie leaning over him for real. The weight on his chest told him his squirrel was sleeping on him again. Reid scooted off when he tried to sit up, and the squirrel ran up the leg of the table. Aidan realized he truly couldn't move, and looked down to see his hands tied together with rope and his feet tied as well. He was naked, having made love to Effie during the night.

"What are ye doin' to me, angel?" he asked in surprise.

"I'm . . . tying you up," she said, looking away from him quickly, but not before he saw a tear in her eye.

"I dinna understand."

"I didna think ye would."

"Och, lassie," he said with a chuckle and lay his head back down on the stone. "Ye want te make love te me tied up, dinna ye? I tried this once with a hoor and it was verra excitin'."

"Nay, Aidan. Thet's no' it, and I'm sorry but I haveta gag ye too, so ye dinna call out fer Kyla." She stuffed a rag in his mouth and tied it around the back of his head.

He tried to tell her that his angel was being a little devil and it excited him, but the words didn't come out since his mouth was gagged. He figured he'd let her do what she wanted with him, as he was always up for something new when it came to games involving coupling.

"I'm sorry, Aidan, and I only wish this coulda been different. But I'm sure ye will jest find another lassie te say ye love on the morrow. Me sister needs me and I have no choice."

"Yer sither?" he said through the gag, wondering what she meant, since she'd told him her sister was dead. He felt a knot in his stomach and a sickening sense suddenly overtaking him that she'd been lying. Aye, he had the awful feeling something was horribly wrong, and that this was not a love game after all.

The door to the room burst open, and like in his dream, the English soldiers marched in.

"Where is it?" Aidan recognized the Scottish man leading the soldiers into the room. He was the man that Effie said was a gypsy in her clan. The one they'd left back in Glasgow. He pushed his way forward, knocking over a chair in the process. "Where is the Stone o' Destiny?"

Stone of Destiny? This couldn't be happening. Aidan shook his head, willing this vision to leave, hoping it was still part of his dream. Effie couldn't really be a traitor, could she? And after he'd brought her straight to the stone. He prayed he was mistaken, but when he looked back toward her and saw the tears streaming down her face, he knew that he'd misjudged her.

He should have listened to his friends from the very beginning, and never have trusted her. Now he knew what his dream meant. She wasn't his dream angel after all. The tail she had in his dream should have made it obvious, but he was so infatuated with her that he didn't want to believe it. She was a traitor, his enemy. Someone who'd only used him to get to the stone. Aye, his dream was turning into a nightmare of the worst kind.

"Naaaaaay!" came Aidan's muffled cry as he struggled to sit up. He rolled over on the pallet, reaching his tied hands for his sword that was lying on the chair. Effie rushed over and picked it up before he could get it. She turned it around with the heavy hilt of the sword facing him, and for a split second he thought she was handing it to him or going to help. But then his angel did something he never expected. She raised the hilt of the sword up high and brought it crashing down against his skull.

The last thing he heard was Reid scolding her from somewhere in the room, and then he saw stars as his eyes closed and his world blackened in front of him.

EFFIE'S HEART broke at what she'd just done to Aidan, and she threw down his sword and fell to her knees crying.

"Where's the stone?" asked Tasgall again, shaking her by the shoulders.

"It's under his heid!" she cried out. "He uses it as a pillow."

Tasgall and one of the guards rolled Aidan's body off the pallet, and he landed right in front of her. She reached down and slowly touched him on the head, noticing the big bump and blood that accompanied the gash she'd given him.

She tore off a piece of her skirt and wrapped it around his head. She wanted to take the gag from his mouth and also untie him, but she couldn't. If he awoke in the middle of this, he'd try to fight the English and she couldn't let him do that.

"Here it is," said Tasgall, moving the pallet and spying the Stone of Destiny. He ran his hand over the stone. "It's beautiful!"

"It's a damned rock," said the guard, reaching down and trying to move it. "It's heavy, too. It'll take at least three of us to move this, now someone give me some help."

They dragged it across the room, pushing things aside, making a mess and breaking things in the process. Reid scurried over to her and settled on her lap and she ran a hand over the animal's fur.

"I didna mean te hurt him," she whispered to the squirrel. "I was only tryin' te save his life."

"All right, load it into the cart," said one of the guards from behind her.

She reached over to Aidan's clothes and laid them over him to cover his naked body. It pained her to know she would never feel his arms around her or his body pressed up against hers ever again. She wanted nothing more than to cuddle up with him and make love all night long or to dance with him or just sit there and talk, but that was all over now. The worse part was, that she didn't know if it really meant anything to him after all.

"Get his weapons," she heard one of the guards call out. She quickly palmed his dirk and hid it beneath the pallet just under his leg. She couldn't leave him defenseless.

Two guards rushed over and grabbed his weapons, and another pilfered things in the cottage and stuck them into his pouch. Then yet another guard walked over and dragged her to her feet.

"Come on," said the guard, "we may need you."

"What should we do with the Highlander?" asked the man who was stealing whatever he could get his hands on.

"Just kill him," snapped the guard holding her arms and dragging her to the door.

She broke free from him and rushed back to Aidan and threw herself down to cover his body.

"Ye'll have te kill me first," she said, refusing to move out of the way. She wanted to leave some sort of sign for Aidan. To let him know she didn't really want to betray him, but had no choice. She saw her brooch under the edge of the pallet where she'd put it earlier, and picked it up and hid it in his bound hands so the guards wouldn't see it and take that too. Hopefully, this would give Aidan some sort of message.

"Let's go," shouted Tasgall from the door. "The longer we wait the more chance the clan will return and catch us. The stone is in the wagon, now bring the lassie and hurry up about it already."

"Come on," said the guard who was going to kill Aidan, and he put away his sword. "He's not going to come after us without any weapons or clothes." He reached down and tore the clothes away from atop Aidan's body, and dragged Effie out the door. Laughing, he threw Aidan's clothes onto the back of the cart with the stone. Then they pushed her onto the front of the wagon, and Tasgall slapped the reins against the horse and sped away, following the guards.

She looked back one last time as they left, and saw Kyla walking up from the loch. The girl saw her in the distance, and Effie turned around quickly, hoping Kyla wouldn't call out for her.

"What are ye lookin' at?" asked Tasgall, starting to turn around.

"Nothin', now let's move faster already." She reached out and grabbed the reins and urged the horse forward. The cart jolted and Tasgall fell backwards, and Effie got the horse to move so fast, that they passed up the guards. She could only hope they hadn't spotted Kyla, and that Tasgall wouldn't say that he'd seen her.

The only thing that made her feel better was that she knew Kyla would be there for Aidan when he awoke. She tried to dismiss her thoughts of Aidan and Kyla, and focus on how she was going to save her sister. If she thought about Aidan any longer, she was going to want to turn the cart around and head right back to him, begging for his forgiveness.

CHAPTER 14

Q idan awoke to knocking in his brain. He felt like he'd had too much mountain magic last night, and that his head was splitting open. His mouth was so dry he couldn't swallow, and he was so stiff that he felt as if he couldn't move his hands or feet.

The knocking continued and his eyes slowly opened, and he found himself face down on the ground next to the pallet. When he tried to move, he realized his hands and feet were tied and then he remembered that Effie had done this to him right before she hit him over the head with the end of his own sword.

"Aidan, are ye in there?" came Kyla's voice at the door.

He tried to call out to her, but there was a gag in his mouth. What in heaven's name was going on?

"Aidan. I need te talk te ye, wake up." Kyla pounded on the door again and he cursed himself for telling his sister never to enter unless she knocked and was asked to come in. But after she'd walked in on him and a whore at one time, she also wasn't in a hurry to enter if she thought he was naked.

"Kya," he called out, his tongue getting stuck on the gag. "O'en th' dur."

When she didn't hear him and the knocking stopped, he knew he was going to have to do it himself. He pushed himself up on his bound hands, his eyes meeting those of his squirrel as it stared him in the face and scolded him. Something pinched at his fingers, and he moved his hands to see Effie's brooch in his grip. He threw it to the ground in disgust, his body shaking in anger at what Effie had done to him.

Then he pulled his knees up and pushed them under him and managed to get to his feet. With one grip of his bound hands, he ripped the gag from his mouth. Wobbling while trying to stand, he hopped his way to the door. He used his bound hands and took a hold of the latch and pulled the door open. At the same time Kyla opened it from the other side, and Aidan stumbled backwards landing on his doup. Kyla caught herself on the door, and when she saw him, her eyes opened wide as well as her mouth. She turned away quickly and spoke to him over her shoulder.

"I'm sorry, I didna ken ye were in the middle o' couplin', I swear. I thought ye were jest sleepin', especially since I saw Effie ridin' away."

Aidan was furious by this time, and nothing his sister said was making any sense.

"Kyla, what are ye talkin' about?" he asked, using his fingers to untie the ropes at his feet.

"I saw Effie leavin', in a cart with a man. I think there may have been others, but I couldna see thet far."

"God's eyes, what is goin' on?" He looked around the room at the shambles and then his eyes darted to his pallet as the fog in his brain cleared, and he realized what they were after. Sure enough, to his horror, the Stone of Destiny was gone.

"Bid the devil, she took the stone!"

"What?" Kyla turned around, then hid her eyes as she saw her brother was still naked. "Put on some clothes, Aidan. I dinna want te look at me brathair naked."

He rushed over to the pallet and realized his clothes were gone as well. His eyes searched for his weapons, but by this time it was no surprise when he didn't find them. "She took me clothes as well as me weapons. How could she do this te me?"

Reid was playing with something at the edge of the pallet and he realized it was his dirk hidden underneath. He grabbed it and maneuvered it until he cut the ropes that bound his wrists.

"What are ye talkin' about?" asked Kyla, still looking the other way.

"I'm talkin' about thet no guid, gypsy. She lied te me, Kyla. She didna want me at all, though I wanted her. All she wanted was the stone."

He ripped open a trunk and dug to the bottom, finding some of his extra clothes, and donned them quickly.

"She wanted the stone? What for?"

"Turn around sister, and talk te me already."

"Are ye covered yet?"

"I am. God's toes, ye act like ye ne'er saw a naked man before." Then he looked at her as she turned around, and squinted his eyes. "Have ye?" He donned a pair of boots that covered his legs up to his knees. These were usually only worn in winter, but it was all he could find.

"Dinna fash yerself o'er thet, brathair. Like I said last night, because o' ye bein' so protective o'er me, I'm goin' te die a spinster. Now tell me, how did ye get tied up?"

"*She* did it."

"Effie?" His sister was smiling, but he didn't think it was funny.

"She also hit me o'er the head with me own sword."

"How did a wee lass like Effie manage te tie up a big, strong Highland warrior like ye and knock ye out as well?"

"I . . . thought she was playin'," he said under his breath.

"Playin'? Playin' what?" Then her eyes opened wide as she

realized what he meant. "Ohhhhhh, thet. Well, thet's what ye get fer being so adventurous when it comes te beddin' a lassie."

"Kyla, she was a traitor, and I ne'er saw it!" He stood up and pounded his fist into the door. "I was blinded by the deceitful bitch. I ne'er shoulda brought her right te the stone. I shoulda listened te Ian and Dagger when they said they didna trust her. But nay, I was a fool. I thought she was me dream angel. Hell, I even told her I loved her."

"Calm down, Aidan. She musta had a guid reason fer what she did."

"How could ye say such a thing?" He walked back and forth and ran his hand through his hair. "She stole the Stone o' Destiny. She led the English right te us. I was supposed te be guardin' the stone. I've let down the MacKeefes, and worse than thet, I've failed in me promise te Scotland."

"I dinna think she wanted te betray ye."

"The stone tried te warn me, with me dreams." He kicked at things as he paced the room and Reid ran out of the cottage so as not to be hit.

"She would ne'er do anythin' te hurt ye, Aidan. Believe me."

"I told her I loved her, and what a fool I was. She had a tail jest like in me dream. She was me enemy, but I thought she was me angel."

"Aidan, listen te me."

"Damn her!" He picked up a chair and threw it across the room and it crashed against the wall. "I'm goin' after them." He slipped the dirk into his boot and ran out of the room.

"Wait!" called Kyla, running after him. "Ye canna go after them with only a dirk te protect ye."

"Well, they seem te have stolen all the rest o' our weapons. I'll kill them with me bare hands if I have te. And then I'll wrap me hands around Effie's neck as well." He headed to the stable and grabbed the horse Madoc left there, but when he pulled it out of the stall and it limped, he remembered it had gone lame. "I dinna even have a horse now te go after them. What else could go wrong?"

He took off back to the main fire pit with Kyla running alongside him. And he kept on thinking aloud. "If only Dagger and Ian were here, we'd figure out somethin'. I canna believe I asked her te stay with the clan."

"She said she was leavin', but I had no idea why," said Kyla, but he wasn't listening.

"I was supposed te protect the stone and I led her right to it. Now thanks te me, Scotland has lost the coronation stone thet we've hid and protected from the English fer o'er five and sixty years."

"Aidan, mayhap she had a guid reason fer doin' what she did."

"She was a traitor te her own country," he said, looking at his sister. "And she was a MacDuff, can ye believe it? And after her own grandmathair risked her life and turned against her own husband te do the right thing."

"It's no' what ye think, I'm sure. Effie isna thet kind o' lassie, I jest ken it."

"Och, I even gave her MacKeefe clothes to wear. What was I thinkin'?" He couldn't stop himself from saying the same things over and over again. And each time he voiced his thoughts aloud, it only made him angrier.

"Haud yer wheesht and let me talk already," Kyla said, finally getting his attention. "Effie had a sister thet was taken prisoner by the English, so mayhap thet had somethin' te do with this."

"Her sister is deid," he said.

"Nay, she isna deid. She jest told ye thet because she didna want ye goin' after her and losin' yer life fer her."

"I kennawhat ye say, wee sister. Ye make no sense."

"Her sister, Coira, was taken captive by the English. She told me all about it."

He suddenly remembered Effie saying something about her sister right before she hit him over the head.

"I'm sure it was jest another lie," he grunted, rubbing the bump on his head and feeling some sort of cloth around his wound. He pulled it off and saw part of a skirt encrusted with his blood. He knew instantly it was from Effie's skirt and that no English guard would have put it on him. And he did find her brooch in his hand. Mayhap this all meant something after all. He was glad to be alive right now, and was surprised the English didn't just kill him in the process. "Do ye ken where they're supposedly keepin' her sister? If she really is a captive and no' deid, thet is."

"Nay, she didna say. Do ye think they promised te free her sister if she helped them get the stone?"

"I dinna ken what te think anymore," he said, touching a hand to his head. It hurt too much to try to think right now, let alone blink. "Even if it was the truth, she's a fool fer what she did. I assure ye, Kyla, thet the English will ne'er hold up a promise like thet. Once they get what they want, they will no' bat an eye at killin' them both."

"Then ye need te go after them," said Kyla.

Aidan thought about it for a second, and knew that was his only choice in the matter. He had to do something, not just sit there and let them steal the stone.

"Thet's exactly what I plan on doin'. Now give me yer dagger, and any other weapons ye can find. Then go and hide yerself where the English canna find ye if they return. And be certain te take Reid with ye."

"How will ye get te them without a horse?"

"I'll walk all the way te England if I have to," he said.

"If ye'd do thet te save Effie and her sister, then mayhap ye really do love her, brathair."

"Who said anything about me savin' them?" he asked. "I am

goin' after them but it's only te save the Stone o' Destiny and te do me duty te Scotland. No' te do anythin' te help thet traitor, do ye understand me, Kyla? I want nothin' te do with Effie MacDuff, e'er again."

CHAPTER 15

*E*ffie bounced up and down atop the wagon as they travelled. The road they'd taken was not the main one, and it was very rough. Her body ached, and she wasn't sure if it felt that way from travelling all day, or from making love several times to Aidan in the last day. Either way, neither mattered. She still felt disgusted that she'd just started having feelings for Aidan, and then she found out from his sister that he told every girl he bedded that he loved her. Why had she fallen for it? And why did he have to be so nice to her and bring her flowers and food and even give her MacKeefe clothes to wear? Above all, why did he have to be so alluring in bed and so good at his love making skills?

She longed for him, yet she hated him at the same time. She knew she'd never see him again, and she really shouldn't care, but a part of her felt so lonely and empty without him.

"Why arena we takin' the main road?" she asked Tasgall, having hoped they'd see the MacKeefes coming back from the fair. If so, they may have recognized her wearing their clothes, and she would hopefully be able to convince them to help her somehow. But now, with the side trails they were taking, they'd be lucky to come across anyone at all.

"We canna take the main road, ye fool," said Tasgall. "We need te stay hidden from the Highlanders or we'll ne'er make it back te the border with the stone."

"We're in the Highlands," she told him. "It isna a guid idea te veer off the main path. Besides, the wagon will no' be able te handle this rough road fer long with the weight of the stone in the back."

"It's getting dark," said one of the guards, riding back to talk to them. "We're going to camp up ahead at that lake for the night and continue on at first light."

"Guid idea," she said, wanting nothing more than to stop and try to think what she was going to do to not only save her sister, but to save the stone as well. A part of her wanted to just hand over the stone and not care that it stood for the kings of Scotland and their freedom from England. Another part of her kept saying that if she did this deed, all the pain and anguish her grandmother endured for crowning Robert the Bruce against her husband's wishes would be for naught.

They stopped to make camp, and Effie knew that she'd never sleep, as all she could think about was her poor sister in that cage, as well as Aidan, and the look in his eyes when he realized what was happening. It was something that was going to haunt her for the rest of her life.

* * *

AIDAN TRAVELED on foot the entire day, running most the way, making his way toward Glasgow. He had hoped he'd come across travelers returning from the fair, and at least obtain a horse for his travels. However, it was already late in the day, and he knew he'd not come across anyone traveling in the dark.

He was tired and hungry, and had only a sheep's bladder of

mountain magic tied to his waist to get him through the night. He'd left in such a hurry, and was so angry, that he hadn't cared about taking food. He'd have to travel all night long to have any hope of catching up with Effie and the entourage at all.

He stopped to catch his breath, leaning his body against a rock. The sun had just set and the sky was painted in beautiful colors of red and orange amongst the dark clouds moving in. He knew by the looks of the sky and the smell of the air that it would be raining soon.

"Damn," he spat, leaning back on the rock and taking the bladder of whisky from his waist. If it rained and he still didn't have a horse, he'd basically have no chance of ever catching them before they made it back to England.

He took a swig of mountain magic and swallowed it down, closing his eyes and reveling at the taste of fire as it made a path to his stomach, warming his insides and warding away his fatigue. Then, he heard a snap of a twig behind him, and his hand flew to his dagger, but not before he was met by the cold edge of a blade to his throat.

"Give me the ale," a man said in a hoarse whisper from behind him.

He turned his head slightly, and noticed dried blood caking the man's tunic. He could also see that this was an Englishman and not a Scot, and that he was wounded. It seemed as if the man was alone, and Aidan figured he must have a horse to have made it this far into the Highlands without being killed.

"It's no' ale," he said, slowly, "it's mountain magic."

"I don't care what it is, as long as it's potent. Now hand it over."

"Och, I wouldna use potent te describe it, but ye are welcome te have it if ye want."

"Give it to me!" The man grabbed the bladder from him, and Aidan just smiled, knowing exactly what was going to happen.

He heard the Englishman take a big swig, and then gasp for

breath. Aidan reached up and grabbed his arm, twisting it and disarming him, taking his sword. He pushed the man to the ground, and held the blade to his throat now. He could see it was the same English guard who had tried to accost Effie in the woods.

"As I was sayin'," said Aidan, reaching down with one hand and taking back the whisky before it spilled, "I'd call auld Callum's mountain magic the fires o' hell, no' jest a simple potent brew."

"I'm wounded," said the man, "don't hurt me." The sound of a horse whinnying in the thicket brought a sense of relief to Aidan. He'd have a way to catch up with Effie after all.

He noticed the man's bloody shoulder and could see that an arrow had pierced him and part of it was still embedded. He would never make it back to England alive, so Aidan didn't feel bad that he was about to steal his horse. He also knew that no English guard would ever be traveling in the Highlands alone. That told him that this bastard had most likely just come from MacKeefe territory, and was involved in stealing the Stone of Destiny. Now he wondered if he should have saved Effie from him in the first place, or if the whole thing had been staged for his benefit. Effie had most likely been working with him all along. This made him feel even more miserable than he already did.

"Ye didna think twice about tryin' te kill me, yet ye want me te spare yer life?"

"I wasn't going to kill you. I only wanted your whisky."

"Really? And how did ye get thet wound?"

"I was travelling alone when I was accidentally shot by a poacher."

"I'd be willin' te bet thet ye were involved in stealin' the stone, and they left ye because ye were wounded. Now why dinna ye tell me where they're takin' it?"

"What stone? I have no idea what you're talking about."

"Mayhap this will help ye remember." He reached out and punched the man in the face. "Now dinna lie te me again, or next time ye'll no' meet with me fist, but with the blade itself. Now tell me, where are they takin' the stone and what path are they travelin' by?"

When the man didn't seem to want to talk, Aidan reached out and grazed his arm with the sword, drawing blood.

"Ahhhh!" the man yelled. "Fine, they're taking the stone to Liddel Castle on the border. But you'll never catch them, as they've taken a trail that the gypsy told them about that no one uses anymore. You'll never find them."

"The gypsy?" He figured the man was talking about Effie and this made him even angrier that she would tell them how to get to the border unseen.

"Ye bluidy bastard, I should kill ye right now fer what ye've done."

"Then why don't you?"

"Because I want ye te suffer. Ye'll ne'er make it with a wound and no horse and all alone in the Highlands, and I think ye deserve it. Now dinna try te come after me or I swear I'll kill ye."

He punched the man again, then headed for his horse. He was just about to mount when he heard the man running up behind him. He looked over his shoulder to see the man with a dagger raised and eyes wide, lunging right for him.

"I warned ye," Aidan mumbled, turning quickly and raising his sword. With the man's movement forward, the sword was impaled in his chest. His eyes bugged out and he fell to the ground. "If ye woulda jest stayed where ye were, ye may have had a chance o' livin'."

He retrieved his sword, and wiped the blood on the dead man's clothes before unfastening the belt from the man, and taking the scabbard. When his sword was in place, he took the man's dagger as well as the pouch of coins at his waist.

"Thanks fer the information." He got atop the horse and

headed away. He knew the exact path the English had taken now. It was an old road that he and Onyx and Ian had often traveled on when they were younger. It went right along the east side of Loch Lomond, and that's where they were probably stopping for the night. With any luck, he could be there before sunup. He dug his heels into the sides of the horse and sped through the darkness, wondering how surprised Effie would be to see him show up and take back the stone that she'd worked so hard to steal.

* * *

EFFIE TOSSED and turned inside the wagon, not able to sleep a wink all night. She felt awful for what she'd done to Aidan. She knew how much the Stone of Destiny meant to him, and also that he considered himself the guardian of it.

The guards were sleeping around the fire and Tasgall was lying atop the wagon seat. She was in back with the rock. The sides of the wagon were high and the English had draped a covering across it to hide the contents within it. They'd also covered the stone with a blanket.

Effie scooted out of the wagon, and her feet had just touched the ground when someone pulled her backward and held a dagger to her throat, covering her mouth with their other hand.

"Dinna scream or say a word, do ye understand, me black-hearted traitorous angel?"

Her eyes opened wide when she heard the voice in her ear, knowing Aidan had found them. She nodded, and slowly his hand came away from her mouth.

"Aidan!" she whispered, turning toward him, but he put his hand back over her mouth and scowled. There was light from the moon, and she could see the anger in his eyes and also the disappointment on his face.

"I said te haud yer wheesht," he ground out, and she heard malice in his words. It was a side of him she'd never seen before.

He dragged her quickly out of earshot of the guards and into the thicket. He moved so fast that she tripped. His arm shot out and yanked her upward.

She looked up to him, facing him now, and wanted more than anything to fall into his arms and hug him. Then to her dismay, he released her quickly, and when she reached out to touch his arm, she could feel the tightness of his muscles beneath her fingers. She dropped her hand to her side, knowing he had the right to be angry with her.

"I'm sorry," she whispered. "I didna want te hurt ye."

"Enough o' yer lies already. I canna believe ye bedded me only te find the stone so ye could turn it o'er te the English."

"It's no' like thet," she said, but he kept on talking.

"I trusted ye and brought ye inte me clan. I told ye about the stone, and I believed ye cared about it as much as I did."

"I do."

"Ye ne'er cared about anythin', no' even me, though I said I loved ye."

"Ye say thet te all the lassies ye bed."

"What?" He crunched up his face and his eyebrows angled. "I dinna ken what ye'er talkin' about."

"Kyla told me thet ye say thet to a lassie and then ye go yer separate ways in the morn."

"This isna about us, Effie. This is about the Stone o' Destiny and how ye betrayed no' only me but all o' Scotland."

"I had me reasons." Angered by his words, she raised her chin in defiance.

"No reason is guid enough."

"They have me sister prisoner in a cage and will kill her unless I bring back the stone."

He stopped and looked at her oddly, and for a moment she thought he almost cared. Then he just took her arm and dragged her back toward the wagon.

"I dinna believe ye anymore."

"Ye've got te trust me."

He stopped quickly and she crashed into his back. He turned around and looked down at her, and the fierceness on his face was nothing like the gentle, caring, man who'd brought her flowers, cooked her food, and given himself to her as a present.

"Ye betrayed me and tied me up and hit me o'er the head with me own sword, and led the English right to the stone. Dinna e'er say I have te trust ye, because I willna trust ye e'er again."

That cut her to the bone, but she knew she deserved it. All he'd been to her was kind, but yet she'd caused him some of the worst pain of all.

"What are ye goin' te do?" she asked.

"I'm goin' te take back the stone, what do ye think?"

"And how are ye plannin' on doin' that with a half-dozen men guardin' it?"

"Well, why dinna *ye* tell me how to do it? After all, ye seem te be the devious one who kent how te steal it in the first place."

"I willna help ye steal it, if thet's what ye'er thinkin'."

"Ye will do exactly thet if ye e'er want me te trust ye again. I dinna want ye alertin' the guards either."

"Thet stone is me sister's future."

"It's also the future o' Scotland. Now are ye goin' te help me or no'?"

"I canna," she said, crossing her arms over her chest.

"Fine. Then I'll move it meself. But I swear if ye alert the guards, there'll be a battle and I canna guarantee anyone will walk away alive. Including ye."

She watched Aidan replace his dagger and sneak up to the back of the wagon and push the blanket off the stone. He was strong, but moving that stone was more than any man could lift alone. He didn't care. He hoisted himself up onto the back of the wagon and bent down and started pushing it. His face turned red and his muscles bulged beneath his leine, and the stone moved forward slightly.

"Ye're ne'er goin' te move this yerself," she whispered, her eyes searching to make sure the guards were still sleeping.

"Then hop on up here and help me, lassie. Thet's the least ye can do," he whispered back.

Aidan wasn't going to stop until he had the stone, and she knew it would be virtually impossible to move it without the guards hearing. Tasgall shifted from the front of the wagon, obviously having felt it move. Then to her horror, he lowered himself to the ground and started to come their way. They both stopped and looked at each other and They were about to be discovered.

"Give him some mountain magic," said Aidan, handing her the sheep bladder.

She grabbed it without thinking and rushed to the front of the wagon to give it to Tasgall.

"Have a drink," she told him, directing him toward the fire and the other guards who were sleeping. The man took it eagerly, and had only one sip before he leaned back against a tree and started to snore.

She heard the creak of the wagon, and when she looked back she could make out the form of Aidan standing on the ground and lifting the stone off the back of the wagon and dropping it right in front of his feet.

"What's that noise?" asked a guard, opening his eyes.

"It was me," she said quickly, bringing the whisky to him as well. She managed to keep the guards from knowing what was going on, and when they were asleep again, she rushed back to the wagon to find Aidan lifting another large stone into the wagon instead.

"What are ye doin'?" she asked in a hushed voice.

"They're goin' te notice if the wagon is empty."

"They're also goin' te notice thet the stone ye just put in here is no' the same one."

"No' if it's covered and ye keep them from lookin' at it." He flipped the blanket back over it and wiped his hands on his clothes.

"Where's the Stone o' Destiny?" she whispered.

"It's right there." He pointed to the ground nearby. "I need some rope."

"There's some in the front of the wagon," she said, "but what are ye goin' te use it fer?"

"I canna carry the rock back te the Highlands," he told her. "I'm goin' te drag it with me horse."

"What horse? Where did you get a horse? I thought it was lame."

"I borrowed it from an English guard who tried te kill me."

"Was he wounded?" she asked.

"Until I killed him, he was."

"I shot him with an arrow, Aidan. Thet should prove te ye thet I am no' a traitor. No' really."

"Thet proves nothin'. Now get back o'er there while I get the stone away from here. Dinna let them look at the one in the wagon. With any luck, before they notice, they'll be back te Liddel Castle and I'll be far away from here with the real stone."

Far away? He sounded as if he wasn't coming back. Effie didn't want to believe he wasn't going to help her.

"Then ye'll come fer me and me sister, right?" she asked.

By the look on his face, he didn't have to answer for her to know he had no intentions of helping her after what she'd done to him.

"I'm sorry, Effie, but I canna help ye."

"If ye dinna help, me sister will die."

"I still dinna believe ye even have a sister. It's probably jest one o' yer schemes te get me inside the castle gates so they can torture me and try te get me te tell them what I've done with the stone. Well, I tell ye, it willna work."

"Nay, I swear, what I'm tellin' ye is true." She felt the tears welling in her eyes.

"Guidbye Effie. I'm sorry it canna be different, as I really thought ye were the one fer me. Now I can sadly see thet ye are no' me angel."

Their eyes interlocked for what seemed like eternity. She felt the burning gaze of his stare down to her very soul. Disappointment shadowed his face, along with hurt because of her betrayal. She wanted to reach out and throw herself into his arms, and kiss him and feel safe in his protective embrace. She also wanted more than anything to hear him say he loved her again, even if he did say it to every girl he met.

"I am the one fer ye, Aidan. Please. I wanna be yer dream angel again. I . . . I love ye."

She swallowed deeply, holding back the tears. She had hoped professing her true feelings for him would make him see that there still could be a future between them. But he didn't reach for her like she'd hoped. He didn't lean over and kiss her gently, nor did he take her in a punishing kiss. He didn't even say a word.

Aidan just turned to finish the job he'd come to do, looping the rope through the handles on the stone, then securing it to the saddle of his horse. Then he mounted his steed and dragged the Stone of Destiny behind him slowly as he made his way through the woods. In the moonlight she saw his back as he kept on riding away from her, never once turning around. And it was at that moment that she knew she'd lost Aidan forever.

CHAPTER 16

*I*t rained on and off for the next few days, and Effie was cold and tired and felt as if she wanted to die. If her sister's life hadn't depended on her, she wouldn't care right now if her life ended.

She'd wronged Aidan. Even if she'd had her reasons, she should have told him the truth in the first place. Mayhap if she had told him what she was going through, he'd still trust her right now. Or he'd still love her.

But now Aidan was gone, and she'd never see him again. Once the guards discovered the fake stone under the blanket and relayed the information to Lord Ralston, both she and her sister would most likely lose their lives. Still, Aidan just rode away, never looking back. He no longer cared.

The guards hadn't thought to look at the stone under the blanket. Thankfully, because of the rain, they'd decided to keep it covered. Travel had been slow over the muddy, rocky path, but at least they kept hidden from the Scots, so there hadn't been any trouble. One of the guards had always foraged ahead, and when he saw travelers, they had taken cover. Once they were past

Glasgow they had made good time, having gone back to the main road, heading for the border.

She hadn't spoken much to any of the guards or Tasgall for the rest of the journey, and they hadn't tried to talk to her either. Once or twice the guards seemed interested in possibly using her for their manly needs, but oddly enough Tasgall had seen to it that she wasn't touched.

She saw the castle up ahead now, and knew this was the end. She felt a sinking sensation in her gut as she wondered if her sister was still alive or what they'd done to her while she was gone.

The rain had let up, but the day was still gloomy. She wrapped her arms around herself and rocked back and forth as they rode across the drawbridge and into the courtyard. She saw her sister immediately, hanging in the cage from the front of the keep. Her heart about broke when she saw how wet Coira was from the rain, and how thin she'd become. Her sister was curled up in a ball on the bottom of the cage and lifted her head slightly as they approached.

"Coira!" Effie jumped from the cart and ran across the bailey, stopping directly under her sister's cage. "Sister, I'm back," she said.

Her sister's thin hand grabbed on to the iron bars and she raised her head slightly to see her.

"Effie?" she asked in a weak voice. "Please tell me ye found and brought back the stone."

"Dinna worry," she said, trying to reassure her though she knew all hell was about to break loose. "I willna let anythin' happen te ye."

"We've got the Scottish Stone of Destiny," said one of the guards proudly as Lord Ralston hurried across the courtyard to meet them.

"Good, let's see it. I can't wait to give it to King Edward. I'll send the missive inviting him here at once." The man smiled and rubbed his hands together. "The king will be begging me to join him at court after this."

The guard pulled away the wet blanket covering the stone and gasped. Effie just closed her eyes and tried to breathe and didn't even turn around.

"What in God's name is this?" said the guard aloud.

"That is no Stone of Destiny," snapped Lord Ralston. "What are you trying to pull? I may not know what it really looks like, but any fool can tell that is just a river rock."

Effie turned around then, spying the round stone covered with moss and bird droppings that Aidan had used to replace the true stone. It was smattered with mud, and dead leaves clung to it. It was only half as big as the true stone and smelled bad.

"Thet's no' the stone we stole," said Tasgall, and then he looked over to Effie. "Do ye ken anythin' about this?"

"Me? Nay. I dinna ken where the real stone is."

"She betrayed us!" shouted the guard. "She must have told that Highlander to come and exchange the stone while we slept."

"You left a witness alive?" growled Lord Ralston. "What were you thinking? Especially a Highlander. You know you can't trust them. I'll have all your heads for being so stupid!"

"Kill *her*, not us," said the guard, pointing at Effie. "After all, she shot your best soldier with an arrow."

"She shot Dempster? Where is he?" asked Lord Ralston, looking around.

"He came back early since he was wounded," said the guard. "Didn't he arrive yet?"

"You idiot, he's probably dead." Lord Ralston swiped his sword at the guard and managed to sever the man's finger. The soldier cried out and fell to his knees.

"She made fools out of us," shouted another guard, pointing to Effie. And then they all started shouting and moving toward her. Effie backed up toward the wall of the castle and held out her hands, wishing she had a weapon. But the guards had seen to it that all the weapons were kept far away from her.

"I'll fight te the deith," she shouted. "Do whatever ye want, but I swear I'll take down whoever comes fer me."

"Kill her," said Lord Ralston with a wave of his hand. "Kill her sister as well. I don't want to see any MacDuffs in my sight ever again."

One of his guards pulled his sword from his scabbard and walked forward. Effie felt her heart beating furiously and wished she had at least thought to try to at least steal back her bow and arrows from the cart before she'd hopped off. Her sister cried in the cage above her head, and all Effie could think of was what would her grandmother have done in this situation? Then an idea came to her, and she called out to Lord Ralston.

"Stop! Ye dinna want te kill me. Because if ye do, ye'll ne'er find the Stone o' Destiny. But if ye set me sister free, I'll tell ye where it is."

The guard looked over at Lord Ralston who was walking away, but stopped in his tracks when he heard what she said. His head raised and he turned around toward her.

Then he walked back to her slowly, and with a wave of his hand, dismissed his guard.

"I'll take care of this," he said, then looked at her and smiled maliciously. "So you are saying that although we had a deal, you didn't trust me?"

"I – I never said thet."

"So, if you trusted that I'd set your sister free, then where is the stone?" he growled.

"I dinna think she kens where it is," Tasgall interrupted.

"Aye, I do," she said, still holding her hands in front of her.

"Let's find out the truth, shall we?" Lord Ralston motioned to one of his guards. "Get the girl out of the cage and bring her to me."

Effie was happy he was taking her sister from the cage. She

figured she would make up a place where the stone was, and it would buy her some time until she could think of a plan.

The guard lowered the cage with the ropes and pulley, and took a key from his waist and unlocked her sister's cage. Then he reached inside and pulled her out roughly, throwing her on the ground at Lord Ralston's feet.

"Now, let's find out where the stone is." Lord Ralston grabbed Coira by the hair and shoved the sharp edge of his sword under her chin. Coira's eyes closed and she whimpered.

"Nay, dinna hurt her!" Effie took a step forward, but stopped when Lord Ralston scraped her sister's skin and blood trickled down her neck.

"So, tell me where the stone is, and my guards will go get it. But if you lie, then both of you will die."

"It's . . . it's . . " she was trying to decide just what to say, when a low voice from the top of the battlements called out.

"She disna ken, because I was the one te steal it." Aidan stood atop the battlements with his hands on his hips. A ray of sun broke through the clouds just then, illuminating the area around him, making him look like Effie's guardian angel.

"Aidan," she said softly, knowing that what he was doing was mad. There was no way he could take on an entire English army, and though she was happy he'd returned to help her, he was going to get killed in the process.

"If ye want te ken where it is, ye're goin' te have to catch me te find out."

"Get him!" shouted Lord Ralston, letting loose of Coira, and walking toward the battlements. "Bring the bloody Scot to me anon."

A chase broke out, the guards running in a frenzy toward the battlements, and for the moment forgetting about their prisoners. Effie saw Aidan's head disappear behind the tall merlon of the wall as the guards shouted and rushed up the steps. Lord Ralston was making his way over there as well, and she knew

Aidan was doing this to distract them so she and her sister could escape.

"Get up," she told her sister, pulling her to her feet.

"Who is thet, Effie?" asked Coira, shading her eyes and looking upward.

"No time te explain," she said, dragging Coira across the courtyard, and toward one of the guard's horses. "Can ye ride?" she asked.

Her sister stumbled and Effie caught her. She could see how weak she was, and knew this wasn't going to be easy.

"I can barely stand," cried Coira. "Save yerself, Effie, dinna worry about me."

"Nay. I'll ne'er leave ye, now put yer foot in me hand and get atop this horse and make it quick."

AIDAN LOOKED down from the battlements, seeing Effie and a girl that he guessed to be her sister getting atop a horse. So she hadn't lied to him about that part after all.

He had followed the wagon for the last two days, and hid the stone where nobody would ever find it. He decided he couldn't leave Effie with those English curs after all, even if she had betrayed him. He'd watched at night to make sure the guards didn't accost her, and all the while he'd followed in the shadows, struggling with what to do. Before he knew it, they were at the castle. There was no way Effie would be allowed to just walk away with her sister, even if she had delivered the real stone to them. No English lord who was deceitful enough to steal the stone in the first place would keep any promises he'd made to a Scottish lassie, whether she was betraying her country or not.

He was glad Effie figured out what he was doing by distracting them. Now he just needed to make sure the English didn't look away from him until the girls were out of there and riding to safety.

An arrow whizzed past his ear and he stepped to the side, watching it bounce off the stone wall just behind him. "Is thet the best ye can do?" he called out, hopping over the wall of the battlements just as the guards rushed him.

He gripped on to a banner hanging down the side of the castle, and used it to slide to the ground. Once there, he picked up a torch stuck into the wall, and spying a small fire in the courtyard, he rushed over and dipped it in. Then, looking around, he spotted a wagon full of hay and threw it in, catching it afire to cause a bigger distraction.

Once the fire took the attention of everyone and they rushed around trying to put it out, he knew the girls must have had enough time to make it out the gate. He'd left the horse he'd pilfered from the guard hidden just outside the castle in the woods, and he would just sneak away now and join Effie and her sister.

He turned to go, and was met by the end of Lord Ralston's sword.

"Going so soon?" he asked. "I think there's something you need to tell me first."

Aidan swiped the man's sword away with his bare hand, getting cut in the process, and grabbed his own sword from his weaponbelt quickly. His sword clashed with Lord Ralston's as they fought each other, and then to his dismay, a dozen guards rushed up with weapons drawn and he knew there was no way he was going to escape.

"Drop the sword, Highlander," said Lord Ralston, "and mayhap I won't kill the girls." Aidan's eyes shot upward to meet Lord Ralston's, and the man lifted his mouth in a half smile. "Aye, I knew what you were doing the moment I saw you atop the battlements. Did you really think you'd get away with this?"

Then two guards pulled Effie and Coira forward, and Aidan's heart dropped in his chest to think they hadn't been able to escape after all. He didn't want the girls' lives endangered, and so he threw his sword to the ground.

"Aidan, I'm sorry," said Effie.

"Nay, it's me fault," said her sister. "If I wasn't so weak and frail I'd have moved faster and we'd have gotten away."

"Effie, I'm sorry I that didna believe ye about yer sister," Aidan told her.

"Enough with all the sentimental rubbish," snapped Lord Ralston. "Now put them all in cages until we can put out this fire and get things back in order. Mayhap after hanging there like carrion in the sun, the Scot will tell us what we want to know."

"I dinna care what ye do te me," said Aidan, "I will ne'er tell ye where I hid the stone."

"You know, I changed my mind. A cage is too good for you. Put him in the stocks instead," he commanded his men. "Then, come morning, you will be in a wonderful position for watching as I take the lives of one girl and then another, until you decide to tell me the location of the Stone of Destiny."

Aidan was grabbed on all sides by several guards as they pushed him forward toward the stocks, holding his arms behind him. He stopped when he got to Effie, and could see the tears streaming down her face. They just looked at each other and he knew he might never have the chance to hold her in his arms again. She hadn't believed that he loved her, and though he knew he had often said it in the throes of passion, this time was different. This time he knew it was love. If it wasn't, he never would have followed and be willing to lose his life to save Effie – his dream angel.

CHAPTER 17

*L*ooking down from her hanging cage, Effie's heart about broke seeing Aidan bent over and locked into the wooden stocks. His hands through two holes, and his head through another, he couldn't move. After awhile, it would be hard to stand in that position as well.

It was night now, and some of the English soldiers had been drinking, when one of them came by and threw his tankard of ale in Aidan's face. She saw Aidan flinch and close his eyes and grit his teeth, but he didn't say a word. From her position in the cage she could see a muscle in his jaw twitching in anger.

"What's the matter, are ye still thirsty?" laughed the guard, slapping Aidan across the face. Once again, he stayed silent, but Effie knew if she didn't intervene, something bad was going to happen.

"Excuse me," she called down to the guard. "Can ye go inside and find me and me sister a scrap te eat?"

"You don't deserve anything for what you did." The guard was going to torment Aidan again, so she stood in the cage and hiked up her skirt, knowing full well the man would be able to see underneath.

"Are ye sure ye couldna find me a little . . . somethin'?" she asked. It worked. The drunken guard stumbled over to her and stood just under the cage, staring upward, his eyes fastened on her legs. "I'd be e'er so grateful te ye once I get outta this cage, if ye ken what I mean," she said in a husky voice.

"Aye," he said smiling and wiping his nose on his sleeve. "I'll get you something, now just stay right there and wait." Then he started laughing at his own jest and hurried off into the keep.

She quickly scanned the grounds below, not seeing any other guards at the moment. There were a couple atop the battlements, but by the way they were laughing and out of sight, she figured they were well in their cups and probably playing cards or dice.

"Coira," she said in a low voice, "are ye all right?"

"Oh, Effie, I dinna ken if I will live another day. I am weak and hungry and I think I am fallin' fast te a fever."

"Dinna worry. I'm sure Aidan has a plan."

"Is he the Scot in the stocks?" she asked.

"He is," said Effie. "He is a wonderful man. And I willna let him die trying te help us."

AIDAN HEARD every word Effie was saying to her sister. He licked his lips, trying to get the last drop of ale that slithered down his face after the guard threw it at him. Parched and hungry, his skin felt burnt from the hot sun earlier that day. His legs were cramped from standing in this position, and to make matters worse, his nose itched and he couldn't reach it.

"Effie?" he called up to her in a soft voice. "I'm sorry about all this."

"Nay, it is me fault, Aidan. I only wish I could change it all and be back in yer arms at the MacKeefe camp right now."

"Ye do?" he asked.

"Aye," she said. "I miss ye, Aidan. I miss yer friends and yer sister and even thet pesky little squirrel o' yers, too."

"He has a squirrel?" asked Coira.

"Aye, and his friend, Onyx, has a wildcat," Effie told her. "If we ever get outta here, I'll tell ye all about it and ye can meet them all."

"Effie, we are goin' te die, arena we?" cried her sister.

He looked up to see Effie reaching out of the cage and trying to touch her sister. Their fingers almost reached, but just fell short.

"Dinna talk thet way, sister. We'll survive. Somehow."

Aidan could see the love between the two girls, and also that Coira was not faring well from being in the cage in the elements for days now. He thought it was ironic how Isabel MacDuff was put in a cage for helping Scotland, and now her granddaughters were in cages as well, but for helping the English this time instead.

He kept thinking of his dream with Effie and the English soldiers, and how she'd had a tail. He should have realized right then and there that she was trouble. But if he had realized it, then he wouldn't have gotten to spend time with her. He still didn't trust her any further than he could throw her, but he knew that she and her sister didn't deserve to die for what they'd done. It did seem now that Effie was only trying to steal the stone to save her sister.

Coira started crying again, and Effie tried to calm her. Aidan decided he'd had enough of this, and knew it was time to do something about the situation.

"God's eyes, Effie, keep her quiet or the guards will be breathin' down our necks again."

"Dinna be so insensitive at a time like this," she snapped. "Ye have no idea what me sister's been through."

Aidan looked around and when he knew no guards were watching, he shimmied around in the stocks, twisting and bringing his foot up to his hands. He had his dirk hidden in his boot and the fool guards hadn't thought to check him for it.

"What're ye doin'?" asked Effie.

"Haud yer wheesht, before they hear ye. I'm workin' on getting' us out o' here."

His fingers stretched toward his raised foot, and he could just reach it, but not the dirk inside. So he put his leg back behind him and raised it up high backwards so the dirk would slip to the top of his boot. Then he tried once again and was able to just reach it, pulling it from his boot and holding it in his fingers.

The lock to the stocks was just next to his hand, and with nimble fingers, he picked it, and it snapped open. Then he used the tip of the dagger to open it and flip it away, and it landed with a thunk on the hard ground. By using his shoulders and hands, he pushed against the wooden yoke, and it opened as well. He slipped out of the stocks quickly, and made his way over to Effie and her sister.

"Ye did it," said Effie. "I canna believe what I jest saw ye do."

"There's many things I can do thet ye've no' seen yet, lassie, and some o' them I think ye would really enjoy."

"Aidan, no' now," she said, scowling at him and nodding toward her sister, not wanting to talk about coupling in front of her.

"Hold on, I'm going te lower the cage," he said, getting ready to turn the pulley that held the chains securing the cages.

"Nay," she warned him. "'Tis too loud and they will hear it. Pass up yer dirk and I'll see if I can open the lock."

He handed it up to her, just able to reach her. She took it and struggled with it in the lock, but couldn't open it. Aidan knew this was taking way too long, and that they'd be discovered soon. He looked around quickly, checking for guards.

"Stand back, Effie," he said, and leaped up into the air and grabbed onto the cage from underneath.

EFFIE WAS SURPRISED when Aidan just jumped up and caught on

to the cage. He grabbed a hold of the bars and pulled himself up to the outside of her prison.

"Hand me the dirk," he said, sticking his hand through the cage. She did as he told her, and he picked the lock and had the door open in a second.

"Give me yer hand, Effie."

With one arm he held onto the cage, and with the other he grabbed onto her and slowly lowered her toward the ground. "I'm goin' te drop ye, so be careful."

"I will," she told him, hitting the dirt softly, looking around the courtyard, making sure nobody saw them. "Coira, get ready, ye are next," she said in a hushed voice to her sister.

"I'm ready," her sister answered bravely.

Then, Aidan used his legs to swing the cage he was on over to Coira. He grabbed her cage and repeated the process. When her sister hit the ground, Effie ran over to her and gathered her in her arms and hugged her.

Coira hugged her as well, and hid her face in Effie's shoulder, crying softly.

With a soundless entrance, Aidan dropped to the ground next to them, and put an arm around them and hurried them across the courtyard toward the orchard inside the bailey. "Come on," he said, "I ken a way out."

Effie helped her sister as they ran quickly to the orchard and through it, and to the back wall.

"How are we escapin'?" she whispered to him.

"O'er the wall," he whispered back. "There are vines we can climb. When ye get te the top, drop inte the moat and swim across and make yer way te the woods. I've got a horse hidden there. It's only one, but ye two take it and I'll follow on foot."

"Swim?" asked Coira. "Effie, ye ken I canna swim. I'll drown."

"Thet's right," she said. "Aidan, is there another way out?"

"God's eyes, ye canna be choosey at a time like this. Now if ye want te live, ye'll learn te swim. Up ye go."

Before her sister could object, Aidan hoisted her up to the vine covered wall. Effie hurried behind her and climbed up as well.

"Ye need te move faster," said Aidan. "It willna be long afore they realize we are gone."

She'd left Aidan down at the bottom of the wall, but before she knew it, he'd climbed so fast, he was at the top of the wall and holding out his hand to help them.

"Give me yer hand, lassie," Aidan said to Coira, and when she started to object, he just reached down and pulled her up.

"I'm afeard," said Coira, looking over the wall. Before Effie knew what happened, she heard her sister gasp, and then a splash.

"Where's Coira?" asked Effie, pulling herself up to the top of the wall.

"In the water."

"She jumped?" asked Effie, surprised.

"Let's jest say she had a little help," Aidan answered with a slight smile.

Effie looked down to see her sister struggling in the water, being pulled under. She jumped off the wall to save her.

She had just hit the water when she heard a shout from a guard, and looked up to see Aidan in the moonlight, falling backwards off the wall with arrows flying all around him. He hit the water with a loud splash, and she saw him go under, but he wasn't coming back up.

She got her sister to the shore and looked back, but still didn't see Aidan.

"Come on," said Coira, "let's go."

"Nay," said Effie. "I need te go back and help Aidan."

"But they'll catch us," said Coira, as the sound of the guards shouting was louder and she could hear the drawbridge being lowered. They would be out there looking for them at any minute.

"Go, Coira. Run te the woods and take the horse. Dinna wait fer us, jest get yerself te safety. I'll try te stall the guards so ye can get away."

"I'm no' goin' without ye, Effie."

"Then we'll die together, Coira. God's eyes, dinna be so afeard and do as I say already. Take the horse and ride east along the Scottish border toward Northumberland. I heard Aidan's friends say they were goin' te stop at the MacKeefe's other dwelling, Hermitage Castle. Ye'll be safe with them."

"But I dinna ken where it is."

"Jest stay on our side o' the border and head east and ye should be safe. Ask any Scot ye see, and they'll tell ye where te find Hermitage Castle. Get yerself there te safety, and ask fer Ian and Onyx. They are Aidan's friends and they will help ye. Now go!" She pushed her sister, and with one last fearful look backwards, Coira then turned and ran toward the woods.

Effie prayed she'd make it to safety. She turned and headed back to the moat, and dove in where she'd seen Aidan fall. She swam through the wretched water that was dirtied from garbage and dead things she couldn't identify, and then she saw his plaid floating atop the water. When she made her way to him, he was face down. Grabbing him and turning him over, the wound in his shoulder was evident. Looking closer, she realized the arrow had passed right through him. He also had a gash on his head from hitting a rock when he fell.

"Och, Aidan, please dinna be deid," she said, pulling his body to the shore. She was out of breath by the time she dragged him out of the water, and could see the guards heading quickly toward them. His eyes were closed and she didn't even know if he was alive. With no idea how to help him, she felt like she was too late.

She couldn't live without him. She needed him and wanted him and never should have deceived him in the first place, and none of this would have ever happened.

"Nay, ye canna die," she cried, throwing herself atop his chest. Then she reached out and touched his lips with hers for one last kiss.

CHAPTER 18

*A*idan was having that dream again. The dream about Effie, his angel. This time she was kissing him, and she had tears in her eyes. And when she pulled away and turned around he saw the English guards again, but this time something was different. Aye, he now realized what it was. Now, she didn't have a tail.

"Aidan, get up, we have to go," he heard her cry out. Although he felt as if he wanted to just lie there and sleep and not move at all, he heard the terror in her voice, and it caused his eyes to open.

"Effie?"

She turned back, looking down at him, and a smile lit up her face. "Ye're alive!" she said, reaching over and hugging him. He wrapped his arms around her, and it felt good. So damned good that he never wanted to let her go. Then his blissful moment was cut short as he heard the wretched voice of Lord Ralston.

"Well, you won't be alive for long if I have anything to do with it."

Aidan looked up to see Lord Ralston and his guards surrounding them with their swords drawn.

They pulled Effie off of him, dragging her to her feet. Aidan reached out for her, but it was too late, they had her. Wincing in pain from the arrow that had gone straight through his shoulder, he was bleeding profusely and already felt light-headed.

The guards pulled him to a standing position, and he felt like he weighed twice as much with his wet woolen plaid weighing him down. He knew now that even if they did manage to escape again, they'd never be able to outrun them with him in this condition.

"We can't find the other one," said one of the guards.

"Dinna worry about her," said Tasgall, coming to join them. "She is weak and with fever and will be deid by mornin'. Let's go for the stone and get it back before the king's arrival."

"Lord Ralston?" asked the guard. "Should we split our forces and half of us go after the girl?"

"Don't bother," he said. "We'll have the stone before she can tell anyone a thing. Go get the wagon and a dozen soldiers, as the Highlander is going to take us to the stone right now."

"I willna," Aidan said, then heard the cry of Effie. He turned to see a guard holding his dagger to her throat.

"If the Scot refuses once more," said Lord Ralston, "slit the girl's throat."

"Nay!" Aidan cried out, not wanting anything to happen to Effie. "I'll bring ye te the stone, jest dinna hurt her."

"Tie them both up and put them in the wagon," said Lord Ralston. "And bind up the Scot's wound as I don't want him leaving a bloody trail for anyone who may come looking for him. Be sure this time to check the Scot for any hidden weapons, as I'll not have him escaping again."

The guards tied Aidan's and Effie's hands behind them, and Aidan's wound was wrapped haphazardly by a soldier. Then they started pushing them roughly toward the castle.

"Leave her here," said Aidan. "She disna ken where I hid the stone. She is innocent."

"Hah!" spat Lord Ralston. "She is far from innocent, I assure you. After all, she was the one who led us directly to you and the stone in the first place. I can't trust that you won't try to escape, so we're taking her along for assurance. You lead us to the wrong place, or try to fight us or get free, and your little lassie there will be dead before you know it."

"Nay, dinna harm her. I'll take ye te the stone," Aidan told him. "I'll do whate'er ye want, just dinna do anythin' te hurt Effie."

* * *

EFFIE SAT in the back of the cart as it jolted over the rough road, heading in the direction that Aidan had told them to go. Both of them had their hands and feet tied, and Aidan lie in the wagon with his eyes closed. She could see him wince in pain every time the wagon hit a bump or rock in the road.

She scooted over to him, using her knee to try to get Aidan's head on her lap. "Put yer head on me lap, Aidan, and it willna hurt as much when we hit a bump."

His eyes opened slowly and he looked at her. She couldn't read his thoughts, but by his expression, she could see that although he just divulged information to get to the hidden stone to save her life, he still hadn't forgiven her. She needed to do something to regain his trust and also to help not only save his life, but save the stone from getting into the hands of the English.

"Please, Aidan. I want te help ye."

"Then why didna ye jest stay away from me te begin with? Thet woulda been the most help ye coulda given me."

She managed to get him to lift his head slightly, and she quickly slipped her legs under him, cradling his head.

"I'm sorry I wasna honest with ye from the start," she said. "I was scared for me sister's life and I wasna thinkin' clearly."

"Thet's fer sure," he said, letting out a breath and closing his eyes again. "And I wasna thinkin' clearly either, or I ne'er woulda told ye about the stone and brought ye back te the MacKeefe camp in the first place."

"I'm glad ye did," she said, feeling the tears in her eyes. "Ye have shown me a kindness and made me feel special. Nobody has e'er done thet fer me. I will cherish fore'er the time we've spent together." She reached down and pressed a kiss against his forehead and realized his head was very hot and that a fever was starting to set in. If she didn't think of something soon to help him, he would be dead.

"Sleep now, and save yer strength," she told him, wondering what she could possibly do.

* * *

AIDAN AWOKE with a jolt as he was pulled by his feet from the wagon and thrown onto the ground. His body hit the hard earth and he barely managed to keep his head from hitting against a rock as well.

"Arrrrgh," he cried out, feeling the wound on his shoulder opening even wider.

"Leave him alone!" Effie struggled to get out of the wagon, but couldn't, with her feet tied together.

"Set up camp for the night," Lord Ralston ordered his men. "In the meantime, I'm going to get the Scot to tell us exactly where he hid the stone." He pulled out his dagger and went over to Effie. He cut the ropes binding her feet, then dragged her over to Aidan and threw her down on the ground next to him. "This better not be a wild chase you're leading us on, or you'll be sorry." He held the dagger to Effie's throat once again. "Now tell me where the stone is, and I want to know exactly."

Aidan saw the fear in Effie's eyes, and although he wanted to lie and tell them it was somewhere back in the Highlands, he knew he needed to tell the truth. He felt the fever overtaking him. With his wound getting worse, he wasn't sure how much longer he'd live. If they actually had the stone, they might spare Effie's life.

If he'd not been wounded, they might have half a chance to escape. But with the shape he was in, he knew he'd never be able to fight all the Englishmen and survive.

"Jest let her go, and I'll tell ye e'erythin' ye want te ken," he said, trying to make a deal.

"You're in no position for bargaining, MacKeefe. Now tell us, or I'll start by severing one of her fingers, and don't think for a moment that I won't." He grabbed her hand and held it out, and Effie struggled against him.

"Dinna tell him, Aidan. Protect the stone, dinna worry about me," she said bravely.

"If ye hurt or kill her, then I'll ne'er tell ye," said Aidan.

"Then you can just watch as I kill her a little at a time." He traced the edge of his blade in Effie's palm, drawing blood. She screamed out, and it was more than Aidan could watch.

"All right," he said. "Jest leave her alone and I'll tell ye."

"I'm waiting, MacKeefe," he ground out, holding out Effie's hand to make sure that Aidan saw the blood.

Aidan hated himself for doing this, but he had to tell them the truth in order to have any chance of Effie surviving. "It's buried at the crook where the River Annan and the Evan Waters meet," he said, already feeling his betrayal to Scotland like a heavy weight on his shoulders.

"Good," said Lord Ralston, letting go of Effie's hand. She pulled it away from him quickly, holding it against her clothes.

"That's halfway to Glasgow," said one of the guards.

"At least it's not halfway to the Highlands," Lord Ralston answered back.

"Shall we kill them now?" asked the guard. "After all, we know the location so we no longer need them."

"Nay." Lord Ralston wiped the blood from his dagger on his tunic and replaced it in his weaponbelt. "I need them alive for leverage in case we meet any Scots along the way. Besides, I'm not exactly sure the Highlander is telling the truth. But if we get there and don't find the stone, I will kill the girl, I swear. Now untie the girl's hands so she can take care of the Highlander's wounds. I won't have him dying on me before I have the stone in my possession. Watch her, as I won't have her doing anything to help him escape."

"Aye," said the guard, cutting the ropes around Effie's wrists. She dove to the ground and cradled Aidan's head in her arms.

"Aidan, ye didna really tell them where ye hid the stone, did ye?" she said softly so only he could hear.

"I had to. I didna have a choice, lassie," he said, feeling like the biggest failure and also the biggest traitor Scotland ever had. "I did it so they wouldna hurt ye. But if they take the stone back te England, I swear I will kill meself rather than te live with what I've jest done te Scotland. I willna live as a traitor te me country. No' e'er."

CHAPTER 19

*E*ffie had cleaned and rewrapped Aidan's wound, and even convinced the guards to untie his feet and tie his hands in front of him, so it wouldn't pull so badly on his shoulder. She could see he needed stitching, and she was afraid he'd lost so much blood that he would soon be unconscious. She'd bathed his forehead and chest all night long, hoping the fever would break. He'd had ale to sip on, but she wished it was mountain magic for his pain. Still, he looked no better.

It was morning when Aidan's eyes flickered open, and Effie bent over to kiss him on the cheek.

"Effie, me angel," he whispered, and his voice was so soft that she could barely hear him. "I will ne'er ferget ye."

"Ye sound as if ye're sayin' guidbye," she said.

"I am. I'm goin' te try te catch them off-guard and kill them all, afore they find the stone."

"Ye are mad," she whispered back. "Ye canna do it, ye can barely talk let alone stand." She felt his forehead, but he still had a fever. His wound looked bad, and she feared for his life. "Ye will be killed, Aidan, please dinna do it."

"I would die fer me country, sweetheart. Thet's somethin' ye need te remember. Now ye need te escape afore anythin' happens te ye. I'm goin' te tell ye exactly where the stone is, in case I dinna make it to the river. When they go te look fer the stone, ye need te make yer move. Ye canna stay with these English bastards, because they will kill ye."

"I willna leave without ye, Aidan."

"Then ye will die at me side," he said. "Now listen closely. The stone is in the water right at the base of a large Rowan tree. Try to sneak me a dagger and some weapons. I'm goin' te need them te fight off these bastards."

"What are you talking about?" A guard pulled Effie to her feet.

"Nothin'," she said quickly.

"Get up and get back to the wagon. As soon as everyone awakes and we break the fast, we're going for the stone. With any luck, we'll make it there by sundown."

Effie knew now she needed to get away from here and do something to try to help Aidan. If she could escape, she may have half a chance to find some Scots along the way who would be willing to help her. Mayhap they could also save Aidan from doing something that would end up taking his life.

But in order to escape, she knew she needed a horse. She spied the horses tied up down at the water's edge, and figured this might be her only chance. Daylight was just starting to break, and most the guards were still sleeping around the fire. And Lord Ralston was out of view, inside his tent. She knew this was risky, but she had to try. If she were going to do anything to help Aidan, it would have to be right now. She looked back to him lying on the ground, and wanted to tell him what she planned to do, but couldn't. His eyes were closed again, and she couldn't even give him a signal.

"I need to go wash the blood off of me in the creek from tending his wound," she told the guard.

"Fine," he said, "but I'm coming with you."

She looked back one more time to make sure no one was

watching, and headed toward the creek with the guard dragging her by the shoulder of her clothes. He held his sword in the other hand as a reminder to her not to try anything. Once there, he pushed her down to her knees and she pretended to be cleaning herself in the water.

The guard went to a tree, turning his back on her to piss, and she looked up, spotting his sword leaning against a rock behind him. She quickly got to her feet and walked quietly to get it. Then she picked up the sword in two hands and lifted it above her head and rushed toward him. He turned just as she plunged the sword downward, and it embedded itself into his chest. His wide eyes looked up to her in surprise and he fell backwards onto the ground – dead.

Effie's whole body shook at what she'd just done. She'd killed a man, and now she knew she had to escape or they'd kill her in return. She placed her foot on the man's chest and pulled the blade from his body and threw it to the ground. Then she took hold of his feet and dragged him into the water. The flow of the stream took his body, sending him floating away. Mayhap she'd be able to get away with this after all.

But all hopes were dashed when she turned around and bumped directly into Tasgall.

CHAPTER 20

"Tasgall!" She felt her world crashing down around her. "What were ye thinkin', lass?"

"I . . . I had no choice. He tried to attack me."

"I saw the whole thing. His back was turned te ye. Ye killed him in cold blood."

"And I'd do it again," she retorted, rushing forward and picking up the sword from the ground, gripping it tightly in her hands. She raised it and pointed it at him. "I'll kill ye next if ye try te stop me from leavin', Tasgall, I swear I will."

The man just looked at her and chuckled. "I'm sure ye would," he said. "So much spirit in ye, jest like yer mathair."

"Dinna try to stop me," she said, untying a horse from a tree with one hand, keeping the sword pointed at him, the weight of it so heavy that the tip of it was lowering.

"I wouldna dream o' it," he said. "But mayhap ye should take a weapon ye can handle instead. There is a bow and arrows tied on the horse ye are stealin', as I jest readied it meself. Take thet instead."

"What kind o' trick is this?" she asked him. "I ken ye are up te somethin'."

"I was goin' te make an escape meself this mornin', but ye beat me to it."

"Thet makes no sense. Ye are one o' them."

"Effie, I admit I did what I had to in order te survive when the English attacked our camp. I made the mistake o' befriendin' some o' them and I accidentally told them about ye being one o' the original MacDuffs, and all about yer mathair and grand-mathair."

"Ye bastard! 'Tis yer fault then that the whole gypsy clan is deid and also thet the English are about te steal the Stone o' Destiny."

"Nay, the fact they found the stone is yer fault, lassie, tho I dinna feel guid about what I did either."

"Thet's no' true. Ye were helpin' them all along."

"If ye didna notice, I was also helpin' ye and Coira. If it wasna fer me interferrin', ye'd both be defiled, and yer precious High-lander as well as the Scottish lassie I saw at the camp would be deid."

She thought about this. He had seemed to step in more than once and sway the English from doing exactly what he just said. He'd told them not to waste time killing Aidan, nor did he say a word about seeing Kyla. Still, she didn't trust him.

"If ye werena helpin' the English then ye woulda done some-thin' te help me and Aidan escape by now. Instead, ye were only tryin' te save yer own neck."

"I admit, I was tempted te be on their side, Effie. It was the Comyn bluid in me thet swayed me te temptation. But I ne'er wanted it te come te this, I swear."

"Then do somethin' te try te change the outcome instead o' bein' such a coward. Think o' someone else besides yerself fer a change."

"Like ye're doin'?" he asked. "I see ye tryin' te save yer own neck as well."

"I'm tryin' te save Aidan's life and also the stone from gettin' inte the hands o' the English. Now if ye truly did have a change o' heart, then ye'll help me escape and find help."

"Ye're right," he said. "I've been a coward me whole life, and now thet I see how brave ye are, I feel even worse."

"Then stop all the clishmaclaver, and get on a horse and come with me."

"Nay," he said with a shake of his head and she thought he was going to turn her over to the English after all. "I canna do thet. I am goin' te stay here and do what I can te help Aidan as well as te help save the Stone o' Destiny. Ye go on and ride fer help. I'm goin' te pretend I am still on their side until I think o' somethin' that'll fix all this. I'll try te stall fer time and I'll think up an excuse why they shouldna go after ye. Now hurry, and get goin' afore they see ye."

"Ye may want te try te sneak this sword te Aidan," she said, handing it to him and getting atop the horse. "After all, he is so mad he plans on tryin' te kill off all the soldiers, even with a wounded shoulder and with hands thet are tied together."

"Ye two are in love, arena ye?"

"I do love him, Tasgall, though unless I redeem meself in his eyes, he'll ne'er see me as anythin' but a traitor."

"I once loved yer mathair, Effie, though she ne'er even kent it. I was too much a coward te e'er tell her how I felt about her."

"So thet's what's behind yer change o' heart," she said.

"Aye," he said with a slight nod, "I suppose so. I've made a lot o' mistakes in me life, and afore I leave this world, I need te do at least one guid thing. And I want thet te be savin' the love between ye and Aidan."

He looked up quickly, and she thought she heard movement from the camp as well. "Go, quickly," he told her, "and dinna look back, lass. Find help as soon as ye can, or all o' this will soon be fer nothin'."

She nodded to him and then took off through the forest atop the horse, knowing now that what Tasgall had done had been no worse than her own actions. If Tasgall could change, then so could she. She would not let the MacDuff name go down in history as being traitorous after all. And she would do whatever it took to redeem herself in Aidan's eyes, because if not, she would be losing forever the only man she'd ever loved.

AIDAN LOOKED up to see Effie riding away on a horse, and felt relieved that she'd heeded his warning and was escaping. It was a weight off his shoulders that he wouldn't have to worry about her being killed now when he attacked the soldiers. He knew what he had to do. If they didn't go after her and catch her, then he knew she'd be safe and he could continue with his plan to save the stone.

His heart was saddened by the fact he'd never see her again, as he was sure he was going to die trying to keep the English from getting their hands on the Stone of Destiny. But he was the guardian and he'd failed in his duties. He would try one last time to right a wrong, and would go to his death trying to keep one of Scotland's biggest secrets.

CHAPTER 21

*E*ffie rode like the wind, looking over her shoulder once more. The English guards had been following her for the last hour, but she'd veered off the trail and stuck to the creek, making her way towards Hermitage Castle. It wasn't far and if she could make it there quickly, she might have half a chance of helping Aidan.

Then, after traveling for another hour or so and not seeing the soldiers following her anymore, she decided to stop and cool off and water her horse.

She had just bent down and splashed water on her face when she heard a noise of an animal from the thicket behind her. Her horse reared up, scared, and she jumped up to grab its reins, but it took off in the opposite direction.

"God's teeth, I dinna have time fer this," she said aloud, and turned to go after the horse, but stopped dead in her tracks when she was met head on by a Scottish wildcat. She froze, her heart skipping a beat, as the animal put its head lower and moved toward her. She wished now that she'd removed the bow and arrows from the horse. At least then, she'd be able to kill this animal before it attacked her. It might be small, but it was hissing and showing some very sharp teeth.

She stepped backwards slowly, meaning to run, and that's when she heard a voice call out.

"Tawpie, get yer doup o'er here," came a voice she recognized as Onyx's. Then, through the thicket she saw Aidan's friends, Onyx and Ian, riding their horses toward her.

"Effie?" called out Ian, jumping from his horse and running to her. She looked over her shoulder at the wildcat once more, and then ran to him, burying herself in his arms. She couldn't hold back the tears, and started crying.

"Dinna fret about the cat," said Ian. "Thet's Dagger's pet, Tawpie. She willna harm ye."

"I am so glad te see ye two," she said. "And I'm no' cryin' about the wildcat, me tears are fer Aidan."

"He's no' with ye?" asked Ian, looking around.

"Nay. We were captured by the English and Coira escaped, but Aidan was hurt and we were taken as prisoners," she blurted out.

"Take it easy, lassie," said Onyx, dismounting his horse. "We ken thet ye were taken prisoner and thet ye were tryin' te steal the stone te save yer sister. Coira made it to Hermitage Castle and told us all thet."

"Thank God. Then she is all right?"

"She's fine," said Ian, still holding her in his embrace. "Lady Clarista is takin' guid care o' her, so dinna worry."

"Thet's right," agreed Onyx. "And we came lookin' fer ye as soon as we heard. But tell me, where is Aidan? I thought he'd o' saved ye and helped ye escape by now."

The wildcat stretched lazily and then went down to the water to drink.

"Nay, I am here alone as he was wounded and tied up and couldna escape. Besides, he wouldna go, as he told me he is goin' te fight to the deith te keep the English from gettin' the stone."

"Ian and I arena worried thet they'll find it," said Onyx. "After all, we ken Aidan isna daft enough te actually tell them where he really hid it."

"Actually . . . he did," she said with a downward glance, stepping out of Ian's embrace. "But he only did it te save me life, as they threatened te kill me."

"Thet dunderheid," said Ian. "What was he thinkin'?" Then Onyx cleared his throat and Ian looked back to her and said, "I mean, I'm sure . . . he did what he had te do, lassie."

"Aye," said Onyx. "I'm sure he did. And Madoc sent a homing pigeon te the Highlands telling the MacKeefes what happened, so as soon as they get the message I'm sure the rest o' the clan will be on their way te help."

"We canna wait fer them," she said. "Aidan will be deid by then. We need te go help him right now afore he gets himself killed."

"Calm down, Effie," said Ian, putting his hand on her shoulder. "We'll take care o' it."

"Did someone lose a horse?"

Effie turned to see Madoc, Wren's brother, riding up with the horse's reins in his hand from the horse Effie had lost.

"Madoc," she said, running to greet him. "Thank the heavens ye found me horse."

"*Your* horse?" He handed her the reins. "I'm English, sweetheart, and I can tell by the trappings that this horse belongs to an English guard."

"It does," she admitted. "I stole it from him right after I killed him, and used it to escape."

"You killed a man?" he asked in astonishment.

"I did," she admitted. "I'm no' proud o' it, but I'd do it again if I had te, if it meant savin' the man I love."

"The man ye love?" asked Ian with a chuckle. "Dinna tell me ye are as crazy about Aidan as he is about ye?"

"Do ye really think he feels thet way about me?" she asked.

"Well, if no', then he's makin' a fool outta himself with what he's doin' lately," said Onyx. "And I ken all about thet, as I was there meself no' thet long ago."

"Where is Aidan?" asked Madoc.

"He's with the English, and they're headin' fer the place where the Evan Waters and the River Annan meet. Aidan told me he hid the stone in the water at the base o' a giant Rowan tree."

"Then let's go get him." Onyx mounted his horse.

"Wait," she said with a raised hand. "First, I need te tell ye thet the Scottish gypsy, Tasgall is no' te be killed. He was workin' with the English, but he's had a change o' heart. Ye'll ken him, as he's the only other Scot there besides Aidan. He helped me escape."

"He disna sound as if ye can trust him," Ian pointed out.

"Well, it's the chance we'll have to take."

"How many of them are there?" asked Madoc.

"About a dozen guards, Lord Ralston and Tasgall."

"Thet is no' a problem," said Onyx. "The three o' us can take them down easily."

"Thet's four te one!" Effie exclaimed.

"Aye, but we'll have Aidan there as well," Ian reminded her.

"He's badly wounded," she reminded him. "Besides, Lord Ralston sends out scouts. Plus, when the guards who were following me return and tell him I escaped, they'll be waitin' fer us te come, I'm sure."

"All right then," said Ian. "We'll take the scouts out first."

"Ye dinna understand. Lord Ralston will be expectin' us. They'll be armed and ready, and will attack as soon as we ride inte camp. We need te catch them by surprise. If we can do thet, we'll have a better chance o' killin' them as well as savin' Aidan."

"Then we'll have to think of a way to get us closer and with the advantage, without them knowing we are there," said Madoc. "And I think I know just the way we can do it."

*a*idan was relieved when the guards came back saying they had lost Effie's trail. Now that her life wasn't in danger anymore, he knew he didn't need to tell them the exact spot where he'd hidden the stone. He'd told them the truth that he'd hid it where the rivers met, but it would take them awhile to search for it in the water. He knew how difficult that would be now that it was getting dark, and that the English would probably wait till morning. Hopefully that would give him time to try to get the stone and move it while they slept.

He felt his fever getting worse, and knew his strength was weakening as well, but he had to try to do something before it was too late.

"Here's the river where you said you hid the stone," said one of the guards, as they arrived just after the sun went down.

"Tell us where it is," said Lord Ralston, but Aidan just remained quiet. They had him tied up in the back of the wagon, and the ropes were biting into his flesh, adding to the pain in his shoulder. His body shuddered from cold, though he could see his flushed skin, as the fever was starting to consume him.

"Speak up!" said Lord Ralston, grabbing Aidan by the hair and pushing his own face close as he spoke. Aidan lifted his bound legs and kicked the man in the stomach, sending him to the ground.

"I will ne'er tell ye where the stone is, and I dinna care if ye kill me."

"Don't think I won't," said Lord Ralston, getting to his feet. He walked over and punched Aidan in the face, sending him backwards and falling flat in the wagon. "Once the sun rises, you'll not only tell us where the stone is, but you'll go and retrieve it for us yourself. If you refuse, then I'll keep cutting off a part of your body until you tell us exactly where you hid it."

Aidan pushed upward and spit in the man's face, only getting himself another punch for his action, this time in his wounded shoulder. He cried out and clenched his teeth, wishing right now he were dead.

"Someone watch the man so he doesn't escape. You'd better give him some water or ale. I don't want him dead before he shows us exactly where he hid the stone." Lord Ralston stormed away in anger.

Two guards came and pulled Aidan out of the wagon. Then they threw him down by a tree. He saw Tasgall watching him. The man had been acting a little odd ever since Effie escaped. Especially since Aidan saw him coming up from the stream as she rode away, but yet he'd told the English he didn't see her at all.

Aidan wasn't sure, but he hoped the man was going back to his roots after all. Because he could surely use an ally right about now.

* * *

EFFIE WAITED behind the tree until she saw the scouts heading out from camp. Then, as planned, she stepped out in front of them in the dark.

"Who goes there?" asked one of the guards. There were only two of them, and that was all they needed for their little plan to work.

"Dinna hurt me, please," she cried out, trying to sound convincing. She could see Ian and Onyx sneaking up from behind them out of the corner of her eye.

"Hey, it's the Scottish girl that escaped," said one of the guards, getting off his horse.

"Grab her and let's bring her back to Lord Ralston," said the other.

"I dinna think that's goin' te happen," said Onyx, stepping out of the shadows and stabbing his sword through the guard. Effie jumped aside as his dead body fell at her feet.

The other guard's horse reared up, and when it did, Ian dropped down out of a tree and knocked him to the ground, killing him as well. They quickly pulled the dead guards off the main path, and Effie ran forward and collected their horses.

"Get those clothes off of them quickly before the blood soils them," said Madoc, coming to join them. "We'll have a hard time convincing them we're all English if they see blood on us."

Effie kept a lookout, with Onyx's wildcat crouching in a tree watching from above her. Ian and Onyx pulled the clothes off the dead men, taking off their Highland attire, ready to put on their disguises. Being modest, Effie turned her head so as not to see their nakedness.

Her heart ached for Aidan and she wanted to be lying naked in his arms more than anything right now. "Hurry up," she whispered. "Aidan's life depends on it."

"Och, this isna goin' te work," she heard Ian grumble, and turned around and couldn't help but laugh. He stood there in the guard's clothes, but he was much larger than the Englishman, especially with all his muscles. The tunic was so tight he couldn't move, and it was much shorter than his leine, as it barely covered his waist. And since the Scots didn't wear braies or hose, that left them naked from the waist down.

"I see what ye mean," said Onyx, having the same problem. He leaned forward, and Effie heard the seams of their tunics splitting.

"We dinna have time fer this," said Effie. "Jest put yer own clothes back on and wear their cloaks and keep them closed in front."

"Aye," she heard Madoc saying. "Wear their helms as well so they don't see your hair and faces."

Onyx and Ian did as instructed, pulling their long hair up under the helms.

"All right, let's go," she heard Ian say, so she turned back around to join them. She looked at them trying to keep the cloaks closed, but their plaids were very visible. And they looked ridiculous trying to fit the helms on their heads with pieces of their hair sticking out from underneath in every direction.

"Well, it'll have te work," she said. "Unless any o' ye have a better idea."

"I do," said Madoc. "You've got an Englishman right here, so use me to your advantage."

"How so?" she asked.

"I'll bring you to them for reward money. Ian and Onyx stay behind us, and whatever you do, try not to speak. With any luck, this'll at least get us into their camp before they figure out who we are."

"We've still got a ways to go afore we get there," said Effie. "What if they find the stone afore we have the chance te stop them?"

"The English aren't going to go digging around in the water looking for anything until it gets light," Madoc said. "Believe me, I know they don't like to get their feet wet either."

"Unless Aidan goes fer it in the dark," said Onyx.

"Aye," agreed Ian. "Then all o' this will be fer nothin', because I dinna think the English will just sit back and let him take it from them."

"They had his hands as well as his feet tied," said Effie. "I'm no' sure he's goin' anywhere anytime soon."

"Och," said Ian, "we ken Aidan better than thet. I assure ye thet no ropes holdin' him down nor the darkness o' the night is goin' te stop him once he makes up his mind thet he's goin' after the stone."

CHAPTER 23

*A*idan waited until the English were all asleep, then he started his plan for escape. If he could just get these ropes off of him, he'd sneak down to the river and somehow move the stone, and hopefully find a way to get it far away from here before they even awoke. He did it before, he told himself, and he'd do it again.

But when he tried fraying the ropes of his wrists against the rocks, every movement brought a searing pain shooting through him from the wound in his shoulder. He knew it was getting worse and he felt as if he were going to retch.

"What do ye think ye're doin'?" asked Tasgall, stepping out of the thicket from behind him.

Aidan was just deciding how to shut him up when the man drew his dagger and came for him. Aidan kicked at him, and Tasgall backed away.

"Stop it, ye fool, I'm here te help ye."

Aidan was leery of the man, but had no choice right now but to trust him. He stopped moving, and Tasgall reached forward with the dagger again.

"If ye try te stab me with it, I swear I'll kill ye," Aidan warned the man.

"Blethers! I'm only goin' te cut the ropes," he said, doing just what he said.

"Why?" asked Aidan, rubbing his wrists, once the ropes were off. Tasgall then went about removing the ones at his feet.

"Because I made a mistake, and I'm tired o' bein' a coward."

"Ye helped Effie escape, didna ye?" Aidan stuck the ropes into his belt, knowing he would need them later. If he managed to get the stone, he'd use the ropes to pull it with the horse like last time.

"Aye," he said with a nod of his head. "And hopefully I can help ye do the same. Now come on, get up and lean on me shoulder. I've got a couple o' horses saddled and waitin' in the thicket."

Aidan got up and leaned on Tasgall, but when they mounted their horses, he started in the opposite direction, toward the water.

"What are ye doin'?" whispered Tasgall, moving his horse toward Aidan.

"I canna jest leave and let them get the stone," he said. "I'm goin' te get it and move it afore they find it."

"Ye're mad," said Tasgall, stopping his horse.

Aidan turned his horse back toward him. "I could use yer help."

"This is nothin' but a deith wish," the man said, shaking his head.

"Well, then we'll both die fer a guid cause, willna we?"

"I'm no' goin' te help. I'm gettin' out o' here alive while I still can."

"Go on then," Aidan said, disgusted, and headed toward the water. Then he turned his head and talked to the man over his shoulder. "And ye said ye were tired o' bein' a coward."

Aidan headed away, feeling like hell. His body was shivering from the fever and his wound was bleeding again. Dizziness overtook him, and knew he hadn't the strength to pull the rock out of the water by himself, but he would at least die trying.

He made it to the Rowan and slid off the horse, tying the reins to the tree. He then slipped into the stream, feeling the cold water biting at his open wound. He hunkered down and felt around for the stone, then his hand brushed across it, and he found it right where he'd left it. He used the embedded handles in the stone and tried with all his might to pull the rock from the water.

"Arrrrgh," he let out a muffled cry as he felt the fires of hell biting at his shoulder. He tried once again, but the rock was stuck in the muck at the bottom of the river and it weighed too much for him to move it himself, especially since he was injured.

"Could ye use another hand?"

He looked up to see Tasgall standing in the moonlight. This was just what he needed, as he'd almost given up hope.

"So ye decided te help me after all?"

"I canna be a coward me whole life."

"And what if we die tryin' te do this?"

"Then I'll die alongside one o' the bravest men Scotland has e'er seen."

* * *

EFFIE NERVOUSLY SHIFTED on the horse in front of Madoc as they rode into the English camp. He held his arm around her, and a dagger against her to make it look as if he were bringing her back as a prisoner.

Ian and Onyx followed on horses behind them, wrapped in the cloaks of the English guards. She just hoped they didn't have to talk, or the English would know at once their little ploy.

"Someone approaches," she heard as they rode up, and immediately, two guards jumped up and pulled their swords from their scabbards.

"I found this girl on the road when I was passing through,"

said Madoc. "Your guards told me you've been looking for her." He nodded toward Ian and Onyx behind him. They nodded back, and Ian almost lost the helm, as it was too small and just sitting atop his head.

"Lord Ralston!" called the guard, and the man appeared from inside a tent. He took one look at Effie and smiled.

"Well, look who's back. Where did you find her?"

"I found her . . . " Madoc was cut short by Lord Ralston's words.

"Who are you?"

"I'm just a traveler passing through on my way back to England."

"By yourself, and on Scottish soil? And at night?"

"Aye."

Effie felt Madoc's arm stiffen around her, and she knew he was readying himself for a fight.

"Guards, is this true?"

Onyx and Ian just looked at each other, but didn't answer, and this obviously made the man suspicious.

"Guards, I asked you a question."

"Aye," they both answered together.

"Guards, bring her to me."

Ian stepped forward and helped Effie off the horse, but when he reached up to get her, his cloak opened, and when he tried to close it, his helm fell from his head to the ground.

"Something's not right." Lord Ralston looked through the darkness, and Ian tried to keep his back towards the man. "Where's the Highlander?" He unsheathed his sword when he realized Aidan wasn't there. Effie wondered where he'd gone as well. Then she realized Tasgall was nowhere to be found either. There was only one place they'd be, and that was at the river, getting the stone.

Before she knew what was happening, Lord Ralston reached forward and pulled her to him.

"Men, we have intruders," he shouted.

Ian and Onyx threw off their disguises, and in one motion raised their swords, meeting with those of the English. Madoc fought from the top of his horse as a battle broke out between them.

"You won't get away with this, bitch," said Lord Ralston, dragging Effie to a horse and mounting, pulling her up with him.

"Help," she cried out, struggling to get out of his hold, but Ian, Madoc and Onyx were busy fighting off several men each and couldn't come to her aid.

"Get the cart and head to the river," he shouted to several of his men, and they took off through the night, leaving the rest behind. Effie had a feeling that things were only going to get worse from here, because she knew that at the river was exactly where they'd find Aidan.

ith Tasgall's help, Aidan managed to get the stone on shore and also tied with ropes, trailing from the back of a horse. They were just going to ride away when out of the darkness and like a bat out of hell, came three riders. As they got closer, he saw that it was Lord Ralston and two of his guards, and to his horror they had Effie with them. One of the soldiers was driving the wagon.

"Och, nay," he ground out.

Tasgall looked up as well, as the English came over the grass right toward them. "Should we make a break for it?" he asked Aidan.

"We canna outrun them draggin' along the stone," said Aidan. "And neither will I leave Effie in their bluidy hands. If ye want to make a run fer it, go. I willna think any less o' ye, as ye've already risked yer life te help me."

The man seemed to consider it for a second, then just shook his head.

"Nay. I am tired o' runnin' and I will stand me ground."

"Spoken like a true Scot," said Aidan, slapping him on the back.

"Aidan!" cried Effie as they stopped their horses in front of them and the two guards jumped off and came up to them with swords drawn. "I'm so sorry," she cried.

"Effie, I told ye te get the hell outta here. What happened?" he asked.

"I came back fer ye, Aidan. Te save ye."

"Why would ye think ye could do thet?"

"Because I have Onyx, Ian, and Madoc with me. They're back at camp fighting."

"They are?" Suddenly, Aidan saw a light at the end of the tunnel. If his friends were here, then he knew he might have a chance after all.

"Tasgall, you bloody bastard, you deceived me," snarled Lord Ralston.

"And I'm proud o' it," said the Scotsman, raising his chin in the air.

"Put the stone in the back of the cart," Lord Ralston instructed.

His guards moved toward it, but he stopped them.

"Not you two, you fools," he said. "The Scots will do it."

"And if we dinna do it?" asked Aidan.

"You know what will happen."

"No' this again," he mumbled to himself as he saw Lord Ralston raise his blade to Effie once again. "I'm getting' tired o' this," he said, taking hold of the stone, and with Tasgall, they struggled, but got it atop the back of the cart.

"Hurry," Lord Ralston instructed. Then when they were finished, he looked at his guards. "Kill the Scots and let's get the stone to safety."

One reached out for Aidan, but even with his wound and with no weapons, he fought like a madman. And when the second came to help his friend, Tasgall jumped in front of the man's sword, just as he was about to stab Aidan.

Aidan looked up to see the Scot lying there with the sword in his back, having blocked the killing blow. Aidan threw the first guard off of him and pulled the sword out of Tasgall and turned around and stabbed the second guard.

Then he spun around and killed the other one as well. When he looked up, Lord Ralston was getting into the wagon with his sword pointed at Effie. She was looking back with terror in her eyes.

Aidan looked down to the dead Englishmen, and then over to Tasgall. He bent down to see that the Scot was near dead.

"I'm sorry I didna help ye save the stone," said Tasgall with his dying breath.

"Dinna worry, I will get it," Aidan said laying his hand on the man's shoulder.

"I am sorry about all the wrong I've done. And now I will die without makin' guid after all."

"Nay," said Aidan. "Ye will die with honor, me friend. And dinna worry, as I will tell e'eryone ye were no' a coward in the end."

Tasgall smiled. "Thank ye," he said, then closed his eyes forever.

Aidan looked up to see Lord Ralston speeding away in the wagon with the stone and Effie in tow. He didn't think twice. He hoisted himself atop one of the guard's horses, and sped after them. When he got close, he jumped from the horse into the wagon, and holding on to the sides, he made his way to the front where he leaped at Lord Ralston, with sword drawn. The man turned and blocked him, punching Aidan in his wounded shoulder. Aidan cried out in pain, and lost his grip on the sword. They both fell out of the wagon and to the ground.

"Ye bastard, I have had enough o' ye," Aidan cried out, just before wrestling the sword away from Lord Ralston, and burying it into the man's chest. When he was sure the man was dead, he stood. Effie had stopped the wagon and came to his side. That's when he heard the MacKeefe war cry of *Buaidh no*

Bas, Victory or Death, from the camp, and recognized the voice of Ian.

"Aidan, are ye all right?" asked Effie, rushing to him. He held out his arms and gathered her up, and then the pain from his wounds and the loss of blood was too much for him. He sank to the ground with Effie in his arms, and buried his face in her hair. His body, burning up with fever shook uncontrollably now, and he whispered to her. "I have ye now, me dream angel. Ye are safe with me, and I willna e'er let ye go."

That's the last thing he remembered before the pain from his wound and the fever overtook him.

CHAPTER 25

*E*ffie pressed a cool, wet cloth to Aidan's head as she had for nearly a sennight, watching over him in his cottage back in the MacKeefe camp in the Highlands. She was so glad that Lord Ralston and his men were all dead, and that the whole ordeal was over and her sister as well as the Stone of Destiny were safe again.

The MacKeefe clan had gotten the message from the homing pigeon that Madoc had sent and they'd come to find them. However, Ian, Onyx, and Madoc, had already killed the rest of Lord Ralston's soldiers and were headed back with Aidan and the Stone of Destiny in the cart at the time. Aidan was close to death, and slipped in and out of consciousness and Effie wasn't sure if he'd ever recover.

With the help of the entire clan, the stone was well protected as they brought it back to the Highlands. At Effie's request, they'd placed it under Aidan's head as he slept. She hoped he'd have some sort of a dream that would wake him and bring him back to her already.

Aidan's pet squirrel nudged him with its nose, it's furry little red head moving back and forth obviously wondering why Aidan wasn't petting him. Then it carefully crawled atop Aidan's chest and curled up into a ball, making small noises.

"I ken ye're worried, Reid." Effie ran a hand over its fur. "So am I."

The door to the cottage opened, and Effie turned around to see Aidan's sister, Kyla standing there.

"How is me brathair?" the girl asked.

"No better." Effie turned back around, trying to keep from crying. "He may die because o' me, Kyla."

"Nay, thet's no' true." Kyla rushed in and fell to her knees next to Effie. "Me brathair is strong and has been in many worse situations. He'll pull through, Effie, jest give him some time."

Effie reached out and ran her fingers lightly across the stitches in Aidan's shoulder. "Ye are so strong, Kyla, and I admire ye fer it. And I only hope ye're right about yer brathair. Ye ken Madoc was kind enough to sew up his wound afore he left, but he needed te go as his wife is havin' a bairn."

"I ken," said Kyla.

"I woulda liked te have had bairns with Aidan some day. I wish thet things woulda worked out differently."

"Ye ne'er ken what might happen," said Kyla, putting her arm around Effie's shoulder.

"Mayhap ye and Ian will have the chance someday," Effie said with a slight smile. "Where is he, anyway? I havena seen him nor Onyx in days."

"They came te get me," came a voice from the doorway, and she turned around to see her sister, Coira standing there.

"Coira," shouted Effie, running to her sister and burying her in a hug. "Ye are all right, thank the heavens."

"I am," she said. "And though the chieftain and his wife, Clarista, were goin' te bring me back from Hermitage Castle, Ian and Onyx insisted on doin' it instead. They said they wanted te protect me personally as a favor te ye and Aidan."

"The chieftain? I thought that was Storm," said Effie.

"They're both chieftains o' the clan, as auld Ian MacKeefe is Storm's father," said Ian, now standing in the doorway.

Effie noticed the way Kyla's eyes lit up when she saw him. Then, Effie gasped as the wolfhound sauntered up behind him.

"Ian, watch out, thet wolfhound is back!" Effie warned him.

Ian just laughed and reached down and ran a hand over the hound's head. "I ken thet. The thing willna leave me alone e'er since I fed it, so I decided jest te keep it as a pet." Then the hound jumped up and put its paws on Ian's shoulders. Being such a large animal, the hound was as tall as Ian when it was standing on its back legs. A long tongue shot out and the animal started licking Ian's face.

"A pet? Nay, ye are jestin'," said Effie.

"Nay, he's not," said Onyx, walking up and joining Ian with his wildcat in his arms. "And believe it or no', Tawpie disna mind the wolfhound anymore." Onyx held up the wildcat and the wolfhound lowered itself from Ian, and touched noses with it. Then the hound lay down at Ian's feet. Aidan's squirrel was alarmed by all this, and stood up on Aidan's chest, chattering loudly.

The hound jumped up, and Ian gave it a command. "Kyle dinna e'en think about it," he said.

"Kyle?" asked Effie.

"Aye," said Kyla from next to her. She rolled her eyes as she spoke. "He named the thing after me because he said it was jest as pesky, followin' him around all the time. I'm no' sure if I should be honored or disgusted."

Effie laughed at this, and when she did, the squirrel jumped off of Aidan and scurried up the leg of the table. Onyx's wildcat leaped out of his arms and darted into the room chasing it, and Ian's wolfhound followed.

"Tawpie, nay," said Onyx rushing into the room after the cat. It had jumped up on the table and was about to grab the squirrel when Onyx dove to get it, slamming down on the table so hard that it broke and came crashing down to the ground with him on it. The wolfhound jumped atop him.

"Kyle, get back here, boy," Ian said, rushing into the room and diving atop the pile of them on the floor.

AIDAN WAS in the middle of a dream. Effie was walking toward him again, only this time she was wearing a beautiful long gown over a long white billowed-sleeved leine. And over it, not only the bodice but the entire kirtle all the way to the ground was made from the green and purple plaid of the MacKeefe clan. It was pulled together tightly with leathers laces. Her breasts were trussed up in the bodice and spilling over, and Aidan wanted nothing more than to bury his head in her cleavage. She carried a bouquet of heather and foxglove, and wore a crown of tiny purple saxifrage on her head. She was smiling and walking toward him, and when he reached out for her, she moved aside and that's when he saw Reid, Tawpie, and that damn wolfhound running toward him and jumping right at him.

"Nay!" he shouted, sitting up quickly, his breathing labored, his eyes searching the area around him. There was loud commotion going on, and when he looked over to the other side of the room, he just blinked, not believing what he was seeing. Onyx was on the floor with the remains of a broken table beneath him, holding on to the back legs of Tawpie as she reached out, pawing the air. Reid was chattering incessantly, climbing the walls then dropping to the ground and jumping from trunk to trunk around the room. And Effie, her sister Coira, and Kyla were rushing around trying to grab it.

And the most ridiculous thing he saw was Ian on the floor with a wolfhound under his arm in a headlock.

"What's a man got te do te get some peace and quiet around here?" he shouted.

The noise stopped instantly, and all eyes turned toward him.

"Aidan, ye're alive!" shouted Effie, tears streaming down her face.

"O' course I'm alive, but I was deid asleep and havin' a wonderful dream afore ye dunderheids woke me up."

"Aidan, welcome back ye big galoot," said Ian with a smile.

"Aye," agreed Onyx. "We're happy ye pulled through."

Effie rushed over to him and fell into his arms, and when his friends let loose of their animals to come greet him, the squirrel ran out the door, with the wildcat and the wolfhound right behind it.

"I'll get them," cried Kyla, running out the door.

"I'll help," said Coira, following her.

"Aidan, I thought I'd lost ye fore'er," said Effie, kissing him so passionately that he felt his manhood already stirring.

He looked up to Onyx and Ian. "Is e'eryone all right?" he asked.

"We killed off all the English, and lived te tell about it," said Ian.

"The MacKeefe clan? Were they there too?" asked Aidan, thinking he remembered hearing Storm's voice sometime during the ordeal.

"Madoc sent a messenger pigeon from Hermitage Castle, telling the rest o' the clan we needed help. But Madoc, Ian, and I had everything taken care of afore they arrived," relayed Onyx. "The MacKeefes helped us get ye back here alive."

"Thank ye. Thank ye all," he said, looking down to Effie and kissing her gently on the lips. "Where is the stone?" he asked. "Did ye save it?"

"Ye are the one who saved it, Aidan," Effie told him. "And ye are sleepin' on it."

He turned carefully and looked back, now knowing why he was having the dream. He also knew the stone was no longer safe here and that they'd have to move it soon before Lord Ralston's men back at his castle decided to get together an army and come looking for it. He knew the safest place for the stone, and would take it there personally as soon as he was able.

In the meantime, he'd keep guarding Scotland's biggest secret the best he could, and keep using it as a pillow, and listening to his dreams. He kept thinking about the dream he'd just had and knew he'd seen Effie in her wedding attire. And with her breasts trussed up and spilling from her bodice in the dream, he also realized he needed her comforts right now more than anything.

He looked at Ian and Onyx standing there staring at him with smiles, and he cleared his throat. "Shouldna ye two go find Reid afore he's eaten? And by the way, what was thet hound doin' in here?"

"Thet's Kyle," said Ian. "Me new pet."

Aidan wasn't surprised, as nothing his friends did ever seemed out of the ordinary to him any more.

"Well?" said Aidan once again.

"Well, what?" asked Ian.

"I think he wants te be alone with Effie," Onyx told him, pulling him out of the room.

"No threesomes today, Aidan?" Ian asked with a raised brow.

"The only threesome ye'll be gettin' is me arm around yer throat, me foot te yer doup, and me hands throwin' ye outta here by yer ear if ye dinna get out o' here already."

"Dinna fash yerself, Aidan, we're goin'," said Ian, leaving the room with Onyx and closing the door behind them.

"Aidan, I want te apologize fer e'erythin'," said Effie, with sincerity in her eyes. "I didna mean fer any o' this te happen. I was jest confused. I had no one, and I didna want te lose me sister. I didna want te betray ye, I swear, it's jest thet –"

Aidan reached out and smothered her with a kiss, stopping her in midsentence.

"Haud yer wheesht," he told her. "Me achin' head canna take any more of this noise."

"Do ye forgive me, Aidan? Can ye e'er love me again, after e'erythin' I put ye through?"

"I understand why ye did what ye did, but do ye understand why this stone means so much te me, lassie?"

"I think I do," she said, looking down, then nodding. "Aye, I'm sure I do. And I promise ye, Aidan, if ye'll take me back I'll ne'er cause ye any grief again."

"Well, now, if thet's the case than ye'll no' be a true MacKeefe. Mishaps and grief are part o' the MacKeefes' lives, but we jest get o'er it all and move on, me angel."

"Aidan, I'm no' a true MacKeefe and will ne'er be."

"Ye will if I have anythin' te say about it. Effie, me dream angel, I want ye te stay here with me and be a MacKeefe. Because as much as the stone means te me, ye mean more to me, and I dinna want te live the rest o' me life without ye. What do ye say?"

"Do ye really mean it, Aidan? Please tell me this is no' what ye say te all the lassies ye bed."

"I've ne'er said it te anyone afore. Aye, I mean it more than anythin', but if ye want te seal the agreement with a beddin', I canna say I'd mind." He flashed her a smile. "I've had a verra nice dream with ye in it, and I'd like te see how it works out."

"What about me sister, Coira? Can she stay here too? We have no family now, and I willna leave her."

"O' course she can stay as well," he said. "I ken our chieftain will give his permission te both o' ye since ye helped te save the stone."

"But it was our fault it was stolen in the first place and ye almost died," she said.

"Storm MacKeefe will understand. His own wife was a leader o' a band o' renegades once and took him captive, so I ken he is verra forgiven'."

"Then I accept fer the both o' us."

EFFIE REACHED over and anxiously kissed Aidan, so happy that she thought she would burst. He fell back and hit his head on the stone in the process, and she proceeded to kiss his head as well. They both laughed, and then Aidan held his stitches.

"I missed ye, Effie. And I couldna even think o' anythin' happenin' te ye. I will be here te protect ye from harm, I swear I always will."

"Make love te me, Aidan. I want te feel ye inside me again."

His hands expertly undressed her while she pulled off the coverlet from over him. He was naked beneath it, as Effie hadn't wanted to risk putting clothes over his wound until he was healed. His manhood was hard and ready, and it excited her to see him this way.

"Are ye sure this willna be too much fer ye with yer wounds?" she asked. "After all, ye are still weak and far from recoverin'. I dinna want ye te break the stitches after Madoc sewed ye up so nicely. He said his half-brathair is a tailor, and showed him how te sew. He was verra proud o' his small stitches."

"Then ye'll jest have te do all the work," he said. "And kiss e'ery part o' me thet is hurtin'."

She reached out and kissed his wound gently, and then kissed his bruised body as well as the scar on his head.

"Is thet better?" she asked.

"I think there's more thet hurts."

"Did I miss a wound?" She didn't understand what he wanted.

"No' a wound, but ye did miss the part o' me body thet hurts the most right now."

"I did?" She pulled back and looked at his entire body. "Where?"

Then she saw the grin on his face and his eyes directed her downward. "I see what ye mean," she said, hesitant to try this, but then decided she would do whatever he wanted. She did as instructed and looked up to see his eyes closing and heard the moan of delight coming from deep in his throat. Not long afterwards, he pulled her up to him and pleasured her as well.

"I love ye, Aidan," she told him as they did the dance of love. It felt so good, and she felt so protected in his strong arms that she never wanted this to end.

"I love ye, too, me dream angel."

"I love it when ye call me thet," she laughed, rocking her hips to meet his, feeling herself climbing higher and higher, the heat between them scorching, and their rhythm getting faster.

"Well, welcome te the clan, Effie MacKeefe."

She liked the way that sounded. It excited her, and she let loose with her inhibitions. While trying to be careful of his wounds, she screamed out when she found her release. He joined her and then she collapsed atop him, wrapped in his arms as their bodies vibrated as one. She had found her man. Her dream come true. And she would be staying with the clan now, and having a family once again.

She would be a MacKeefe, as all the members of the clan called themselves. She liked that. She would try her hardest to gain back Aidan's trust through time, as well as show him he'd made the right choice by asking her to stay. The only thing that could make any of this better was if she were Effie MacKeefe – not just a member of the clan, but Aidan's wife.

CHAPTER 26

*A*idan, Ian, and Onyx moved the Stone of Destiny into the crypt of an unknown ancient monk, deep in the bowels of the catacombs of Scone Abbey. Then, together they covered the stone by sliding the very heavy and tall headstone over the top, sealing it into the ground where no Englishman would ever find it again. Abbot Murray smiled and gave them a nod of satisfaction.

"Ye lads have done guid," he said, sounding very pleased. "Only we, along with King David will ken the new location o' the stone. It'll be safe here until we need it to crown Scotland's next king, as long as we keep this a secret."

"We will," said Onyx, "ye can count on us."

"Aye," agreed Ian, then he looked over to Aidan. "How about ye, Aidan? Will ye haud yer wheesht this time and no' tell anyone where we hid the stone?"

"I promise," said Aidan. "And 'twill be easier this time, as Effie told me she didna want me te tell her where it was and thet she would make sure I dinna tell a soul."

"All right then, I guess our work here is done," said the abbot.

"No' exactly," said Aidan. "I would like ye te join us at the Perth Highland Games, as I am goin' te surprise me love, Effie, and marry her jest afore the competition."

"I would love to, Aidan," said the abbot. "However, if anyone sees me with ye, they'll ken we were together. It's too risky, as we dinna want anyone te ken where ye brought the stone. But me congratulations are with ye and yer loved one, and I wish ye the happiest marriage."

"Thank ye," said Aidan with a nod of his head. "We'd better be goin' then, as I still have a lot te do afore the weddin'. Willna Effie be surprised?"

* * *

EFFIE HADN'T SEEN Aidan in a sennight, and was excited that he was going to be meeting her here at the Highland Games in Perth today. She'd been here since this morning with the MacKeefe clan, and even Storm's parents were present. Kyla had introduced her to them this morning.

Effie sat back on the grass, overlooking the open fields and rolling green hills, as well as the high mountains in the distance. Beautiful purple and pink heather spilled down the valleys, and the skies above it were bright blue. She'd never seen such a beautiful sight in her life.

Her sister was picking wildflowers with Kyla, and looked up and waved at her. Effie smiled and waved back. Coira's health was improving every day, and it did Effie good to see her sister smile again after everything she'd been through. Her sister no longer seemed so frail or afraid. She'd made friends with Kyla and they were almost inseparable. Coira loved her new home with the MacKeefe clan, and Effie did as well.

Perth was bustling with Highlanders as well as some

Lowlander Scots too, and Kyla had even pointed out that the MacDuff clan was present. She was curious about them, but refused Kyla's suggestion to introduce herself to them. She was afraid if they knew who she was they'd be treating her like a hero because of her grandmother. She still felt like a traitor for everything she'd done, even though Aidan as well as all the MacKeefes had forgiven her.

She just wanted to relax and watch the games today, and bask in the happiness of being one of the MacKeefe clan now that Storm had approved and accepted Coira and herself into their family.

Burly men readied themselves for lifting heavy stones or throwing the hammer, while others prepared for the caber toss.

A long rope was being laid out on the ground, as clans would compete against each other in the tug-o-war. The lassies competed in their own events, and Effie knew that Kyla had been practicing tossing the sheaves with a pitchfork high into the air for the last month back at camp. She was trying her hardest to impress Ian.

The children of the clans competed in their smaller versions of the games as well as a footrace.

Bagpipes split the air, and drumming joined in, signaling that the competition would start soon. The smell of mutton pie and haggis drifted lazily through the air, making her hungry, but she was waiting for Aidan before she had anything to eat.

Then, she saw Onyx and Ian riding toward her, and her heart skipped a beat as she shaded her eyes from the sun, eagerly looking for Aidan.

"Lookin' fer me?" Two hands snaked around her waist from behind, and Aidan nuzzled his face into the crook of her neck, kissing her.

"Aidan! Ye're back." She jumped up and turned around and threw herself into his arms. "I missed ye."

"I missed ye as well," he said, kissing her again. "I brought ye a present."

"A present? Fer me?" she asked, then raised an eyebrow and grinned devilishly. "Well, if it's anythin' like me birthday present, then mayhap we'd better wait till we are at least under the cover o' some trees."

"It's no' thet," he said, "no' now anyway. But I promise ye we'll have some o' thet later."

He walked over to his horse and pulled something out of a travel bag, and handed it to her. She took it gingerly in her hands and opened the bundle to see the most beautiful gown made entirely of the MacKeefe purple and green plaid, with a white leine with billowy sleeves to wear beneath it. The bodice was laced with purple and green braided ribbons, and there was a matching circlet for her head as well.

"It's beautiful, Aidan. Where did ye get it?"

"I had Madoc's step-brathair who is a tailor make it fer ye. Madoc may be handy with a needle when it comes te closin' up a wound, but his step-brathair, William, is a Master Tailor, so I hired him te do it. It is constructed so well it'll last ye a lifetime. Ye ken, William even has his own shop and belongs te the guild."

"Why would ye hire him te make this, when I already have clothes te wear?" she asked, feeling like something good was about to happen.

"I did it so ye'd have somethin' special te wear today. Somethin' thet is yers and no' borrowed from someone else."

"Fer the Highland Games?" she asked. "I dinna understand."

"Effie," he said, pulling something from the pouch at his waist. "I have somethin' else te give ye as well. I've been thinkin' about this fer a long time now, and I hope ye'll say yes."

"Say yes?" She was sure now that something good was about to happen. And when Aidan got down on one knee and took her hands in his, she knew she hadn't been mistaken.

"Effie, say ye'll marry me and be me wife. I love ye, me dream angel." He opened his fist and there was a ring. A shiny, gold ring with an amethyst stone, and angels etched into the band.

Tears welled in her eyes and her throat tightened and she felt as if she couldn't speak. She nodded her head furiously, and then choked out the words, "I will, Aidan. I will be yer wife. I love ye, too."

She sank to her knees and fell atop him, kissing him as they rolled to the ground.

"The priest is here as well, Effie," he said. "We can get married right here, right now."

"I'd like thet," she said.

"I brought yer grandmathair's brooch, too. I was hopin' thet ye would wear it when I bring ye te meet the MacDuffs today."

"Nay, Aidan, I canna. I dinna deserve the brooch nor te meet the MacDuffs after I was te blame fer Scotland almost losin' the Stone o' Destiny fore'er."

"They dinna ken thet, angel. Only the MacKeefes ken the truth, and we are all goin' te keep quiet about thet, I assure ye."

"But I'm afeard. I dinna ken any o' them. They are strangers te me."

"Then I'll be there by yer side when ye and yer sister meet the MacDuffs. And ye'll have nothin' te fret about because ye'll be there as me wife."

"All right," she said nervously. "I'll meet them, Aidan. No' fer me, but fer Coira. She's ne'er even kent her own mathair nor her faither, so I think ye're right and this is important.

"Then put on the gown, me angel, and let's go get married."

CHAPTER 27

MadMan MacKeefe Series

$\mathcal{E}$ffie felt like the luckiest girl in the world as Aidan slipped the ring on her finger just as they'd finished their vows. She wore her new gown that matched Aidan's plaid. Her sister stood next to her, holding the bouquet of wildflowers she and Kyla had picked for her this morning, and Kyla was next to her, crying happy tears. Onyx and Ian stood alongside Aidan, while Storm, Wren, and the entire MacKeefe clan as well as the MacDuffs watched on.

Aidan had convinced her to meet the MacDuffs before they were married, so they could be present at the wedding as well. It had gone better than she'd hoped and she'd even found a few blood relatives she never knew she had. Coira enjoyed meeting them as well, and now Effie felt as if they had two families.

Madoc had brought his wife, Abbey, and their new baby boy, as well as their other two children to the competition as well. Onyx's wife, Lovelle, stood next to them with their new baby boy, Creighton, in her arms. They had given him a Scottish name at Onyx's insistence. And Onyx had even brought his father, Talbot, from England, so he could be with Onyx's Scottish family.

"I pronounce ye husband and wife," said the priest, closing his book.

A shout went up from the crowd, and Aidan reached over and kissed Effie, then lifted her off her feet and kissed her again.

"Congratulations," said Storm, coming to greet them. With that, congratulations and hugs and kisses were given all around.

"Jest because ye're a married man now, Aidan, thet disna mean ye can beat me in the caber toss," said Storm.

"Me wounds are healing nicely, and I feel strong as an ox today," said Aidan, winking at Effie.

Renard walked up with Niall at his side, holding on to Aidan's squirrel.

"The games are starting," he said. "There are competitors here from at least a dozen clans."

"Let's go," said Ian, then he looked back to Renard and Niall. "Are ye two sure ye can hold on te Reid, Kyle, and also Tawpie throughout the games?"

"Aye," said Niall. "We have yer wolfhound and wildcat tied on leads, so they willna cause trouble."

"Guid," said Onyx, putting his arm around his wife and coming to join them. "There are a lot o' bairns here today and we dinna want trouble."

"No one is goin' anywhere afore we've made a toast te the new couple with some o' me mountain magic," said old Callum MacKeefe who had come from his pub in Glasgow to join them. He nodded his head, and several clanmembers passed out wooden cups and filled them with the potent whisky.

"Grandda," said Storm, holding his youngest daughter, Heather, in one arm, and a cup of mountain magic in the other, "ye make the first toast."

"All right," said Callum. "I toast te Aidan and Effie and thet they will have plenty o' laddies te drink me mountain magic."

"I toast te them as well," said Kyla, holding her cup in the air. "Thet they will have plenty o' lassies te drink it, too."

Cheers and laughter went up from the crowd, and everyone drank to the toasts.

"Kyla," said Ian, downing his whisky and smacking his lips. "Ye ken thet lassies canna really drink this, so dinna even pretend they can."

"Oh no?" She looked at him and smiled, then raised the cup to her lips.

"Dinna do it," said Effie, remembering the last time she had tried this herself.

"Dinna worry, Effie," Kyla assure her. "Since Ian thinks o' me as one o' the boys, this shouldna affect me." She downed it, made a face, and then a smile widened her lips. "Ye see, Ian, ye are no' the only one thet can drink mountain magic. And if ye'd like te watch me, I am goin' te win the sheaf toss as well."

"She surprised me," said Effie, as the crowd headed over to the games. "I dinna ken how she does it."

"She is me sister," said Aidan. "She has been followin' me and me friends around her entire life and tryin' te be one o' the laddies I think."

"Och, I think it's much more than thet," said Effie, watching Ian and Kyla arguing about who was better at everything as they headed toward the games.

"Come on, Aidan," said Storm, "the caber toss is startin' soon, and I willna be givin' up me title."

* * *

EFFIE SAT TO THE SIDE, watching the competition all day, glancing at her ring from time to time, hardly able to believe that she was now married. She felt so happy, and like she actually belonged with the MacKeefes, and she was looking forward to getting to know the MacDuffs better as well. She ran a loving hand over the brooch pinned to her shoulder, wishing she would have had the opportunity of knowing her grandmother, Isabel MacDuff. She also wished her mother had still been alive and that she could have been here for her wedding. She knew her mother would have loved Aidan.

Coira sat next to her as well as Wren, and Onyx's wife Lovelle, and Madoc's wife, Abbey. Their many children were gathered around, and had even participated in some of the children's competitions. Heather, Storm's young daughter sat on Effie's lap, while Lovelle rocked her crying baby next to her.

"So, you and Aidan will be having a big family?" asked Lovelle.

"I dinna ken what Aidan wants," she said, "but I would like lots o' children. But tell me, Lady Lovelle, what is it like te be married te a Madman MacKeefe?"

"You will never stop being surprised," she said. "Nor will you ever want them to stop acting so crazy. It makes them who they are."

"I guess ye're right," she said, watching as Aidan finished his second throw of the caber toss, and he and Storm were now tied."

"Wren," she said. "Do ye think Aidan is goin' to be takin' Storm's title?"

"Aidan may have won lifting the atlas stones, like we all knew he would," said Wren, "but I don't think Storm will take it well if he loses his title, so I'm going to have to say no."

Effie laughed. "The MacKeefes are verra competitive," she said. "After all, Ian already won the hammer throw and Onyx the sword hold, and the clan beat the MacDonalds in the tug o' war."

"Dinna ferget, I won the sheaf toss," said Kyla, settling herself next to Effie, and taking a child onto her lap as well.

"This is the first time I've e'er been te the games," said Effie. "I didna even ken thet the women were so guid at the competitions."

"Do ye think Ian saw me win?" Kyla leaned over and whispered this to Effie.

"He noticed all right," she said with a smile.

"Effie, this one is fer ye," called out Aidan from across the field, hunkering down and cupping the tapered end of the pole. The object of the competition was to keep it as vertical as possible and toss it end over end without it tilting or falling back toward the competitor. "Watch this caber toss," he said, and Effie gave the child on her lap to Kyla and stood up to watch, feeling very nervous. She knew how hard Aidan had been practicing to beat Storm, but after what Wren just told her, she wasn't sure if it was a good idea for him to win the title from Storm since he had held it for the last nine years.

Aidan lifted the caber in one jerky motion, taking a step or two in each direction to balance it. Just as he was about to take a few steps forward to throw it, she heard Renard's voice from behind her.

"Reid, get back here."

Aidan's squirrel darted out from the crowd, being chased by Tawpie and Kyle. The squirrel scurried up Aidan's leg and to his shoulder as the wolfhound and the wildcat chased circles around him.

"Och, no' now," said Aidan, trying to sidestep the animals and still hold the pole upright. Then, to Effie's horror, the squirrel scampered straight up the pole and settled itself at the top. "Naaaaaaay," shouted Aidan, and Effie knew it was all over. Aidan was too fond of his little pet to throw the caber end over end when his squirrel was atop it.

The wolfhound growled, the cat hissed, and Aidan lost his footing and the pole tilted too much for him to right it again. Before she knew it, the caber was on the ground without having been thrown, and Reid was back on Aidan's shoulder.

"And the winner o' the caber toss, keeping his title fer the tenth year in a row is Storm MacKeefe," shouted the announcer. The bagpipes started back up and the drums did a roll, signaling the end of the competition.

She looked out to see Onyx and Ian collecting their pets and

Aidan clenching his jaw while he offered his congratulations to Storm.

"Let's go get some haggis, Niall," said Renard and they stepped around the women.

"Wait a minute," said Wren, holding out her arm to stop him. "Renard, did you and Niall let the animals loose so your father would win the caber toss again?"

"We dinna ken what ye're talkin' about," said Niall, his eyes darting over to Renard nervously.

"That's right," Renard added.

"All right, go on," she said, and they ran away quickly.

"Do ye think they did?" asked Effie.

"Renard has always idolized Storm ever since he found out Storm was his father," said Wren. "I wouldn't be surprised if a little foul play was involved here, as Renard has always been a sly one."

"Well, it did look as if Aidan was goin' te win," said Effie.

"Aye, it did," agreed Wren with a nod of her head.

"It's probably better thet he didna win," said Effie. "After all, he already won one event, the same as his friends."

"Thet's right," said Kyla, having overheard the conversation and coming over to join them. "If Aidan won more events than Ian or Dagger, ye ken me brathair would ne'er let them forget it."

"And then they would constantly be challenging each other and payin' no attention te us," said Effie.

"No attention at all." Kyla looked across the field to Ian and crossed her arms over her chest.

"If Storm lost the title, he'd probably be sulking about it for at least a month or two," said Wren.

"Hmmm," said Effie, and they all just stared out at the men. Aidan saw them looking at them and headed their way. "I willna tell if ye two willna," she said quickly before he could hear her.

"Thet's fine by me," agreed Kyla.

"Agreed," said Wren with a smile and three of them clasped hands in front of them sealing the deal.

"What's goin' on?" asked Aidan, walking over to her and putting his arm around her. His squirrel chattered from atop his shoulder. "Are ye talkin' about me losin' the caber toss, me dream angel? Or shall I say, me wife?" He kissed her, and Effie knew how disappointed he felt.

"Nay, we dinna care about thet," she said. "We were jest talkin' about the men in our lives, me husband." She looked up to him and smiled. "Or mayhap, I should I say, me *MadMan MacKeefe – Aidan*."

FROM THE AUTHOR

I hope you enjoyed Aidan and Effie's story. Through my research, I found rumors that the actual Stone of Destiny may not have been stolen by King Edward I in 1296, but instead switched out for a fake, while the true stone was safe in hiding. Instantly, I knew I had to write this into my story.

While the Stone of Destiny that we all know is red sandstone, it is said the actual one was black basalt and had ancient hieroglyphs on it. After all, if the true stone had been stolen, why didn't the Scottish demand that the English give it back, or at least try to get it themselves? Research shows the Scots never even made an attempt to save their coronation stone that meant so much to them. So in my eyes . . . it was because they already had the true one somewhere in hiding.

Now available is the last book in the series - *Ian – Book 3*. And in case you've missed the first book of the series it is *Onyx – Book 1*.

Also, if you'd like to read the stories of Madoc, as well as his sister, Wren, and her husband, Storm, who make guest appearances in this book, you can do so by reading *Lord of Illusion* and *Lady Renegade*, part of my *Legacy of the Blade Series*.

The Legacy of the Blade Series:
Prequel
Lord of the Blade
Lady Renegade
Lord of Illusion
Lady of the Mist

Or if you'd like to read about Onyx's sisters and their romances, you can do so in the *Daughters of the Dagger Series*.

Daughters of the Dagger Series:
Prequel
Ruby – Book 1
Sapphire – Book 2
Amber – Book 3
Amethyst – Book 4

I have included some excerpts for your enjoyment.

Thanks for your support!

Elizabeth Rose

ABOUT ELIZABETH

Elizabeth Rose is a multi-published, bestselling author, writing medieval, historical, contemporary, paranormal, and western romance. She is an amazon all-star and has been an award finalist numerous times. Her books are available as Ebooks, paperback, and audiobooks as well.

Her favorite characters in her works include dark, dangerous and tortured heroes, and feisty, independent heroines who know how to wield a sword. She loves writing 14th century medieval novels, and is well-known for her many series.

Her twelve-book small town contemporary series, Tarnished Saints, was inspired by incidents in her own life.

After being traditionally published, she started self-publishing, creating her own covers and book-trailers on a dare from her two sons.

Elizabeth loves the outdoors. In the summertime, you can find her in her secret garden with her laptop, swinging in her hammock working on her next book. Elizabeth is a born storyteller and passionate about sharing her works with her readers.

Please be sure to visit her website at **Elizabethrosenovels.com** to read excerpts from any of her novels and get sneak peeks at covers of upcoming books. You can follow her on **Twitter, Facebook, Goodreads** or **Bookbub.**

98489298R00119

Made in the USA
Columbia, SC
26 June 2018